ALL I'VE DONE FOR YOU

JOANNE GREENBERG

Paperback ISBN: 978-1-5356-1008-7

Hardcover ISBN: 978-1-5356-1009-4

To Brother Eddie and Ed and all the wealth and love they brought into the world

I NEVER PROMISED YOU A ROSE GARDEN

"A rare and wonderful insight into the dark kingdom of the mind."

—*Chicago Tribune*

"A marvelous job . . . With a courage that is sometimes breathtaking . . . [Greenberg] makes a faultless series of discriminations between the justifications for living in an evil and complex reality and the justifications for retreating into the security of madness."

—*The New York Times Book Review*

RITES OF PASSAGE

"This group of twelve excellent short stories is all the more remarkable for its being not only artistically 'beautiful' but morally and spiritually beautiful as well."

—Joyce Carol Oates, *Book World*

IN THIS SIGN

"A miracle of empathy, a tour de force of imaginative conjecture, and quite simply one of the best novels ever written about deaf people... Writers were invented to produce books like this..."

—Christopher Lehmann-Haupt, *The New York Times*

Contents

ONE
LILY

I DID FEEL SORRY FOR Karen, coming to get me for that stupid party, supposedly a big surprise. No one knows it yet, but I do the surprising around here. I was busy dying so I didn't hear her until much later, after I was fully dead and she had come back with Tim—Sheriff Valken—and all the fuss.

She must have come up the walk to the house, full of eagerness, calling me, "Hi, Mom, it's me"—waiting for my answer. I imagine her moving into the parlor, then the dining room, then the kitchen, still calling, and up the stairs to each room, calling, assuming I'd be resting. I always came home after church to lie down for a bit. Of course, I wasn't there—the house was still. It's my triumph, this old house, although I could barely keep it in repair. It's clean inside and in excellent order. I did it out of spite. The people I got it from were savages; their son, to whom I was married, had been gone for decades. I hope they're all frying now.

Karen must have gone through the rooms, familiar in their order, serenity, and silence. In what had been her room, and Arlie's, her eye might have glanced around at the pictures I have of them, displayed in frames on the dressers and on the walls, their weddings, the grandkids as they came. She had once asked me why there were none of me. "Where are your wedding pictures, Mom, why aren't you standing with your school friends, the Ellies?" Any picture of me is in someone else's house, posed beside the subject of the picture. I didn't tell her that. Now I never will.

Down the back stairs—she must have become conscious of an excess of silence, no air moving that had someone's breathing in it. Her calling would have begun to have some anxiety, and then—of course! This beautiful afternoon, the sky is its ringing Colorado blue, the sun not yet an adversary—I must be down in the garden. It's May. I'd be considering what plants should be kept and what replaced. We're at seven thousand feet here, between mountains of eleven and twelve, and we won't put in anything for weeks yet, but I am nothing if not a planner, looking ahead. I consider. I prepare.

I wasn't in the garden, of course, but it was from the garden that she must have heard sounds from the new garage. My sons-in-law built it for me two years ago. By now I was dead, but not yet disengaged.

I was careful about her finding me—I wasn't horrible to look at, maybe a little too red-faced from the monoxide, but not in disarray—not disfigured—not shot, not hanged. I'd made sure the house was in order and the car spotless and I was in my church clothes. I'd had all the time I needed to do all those things. No note, of course, so the act itself is my declaration of enmity against this town as it was and as it is.

I was born a mile from here in 1932—they didn't know that at the bank. They thought I was sixty-five. There's an advantage to being born at home when home is the south side of Hungry Mother Mountain. I have no birth certificate, which worked very well when I finally registered my birth. I gave myself two extra years.

Karen opened the garage door and saw me and stopped feeling or thinking, but she opened the car door and sensibly reached over me and shut off the motor. I couldn't understand what sounds she was making.

There was a pleat in time and when my vision cleared Tim Valken was there. He is sheriff, now. His father and I went to school together, and I had a flickering little crush on Bobby Valken. Bobby was a little too friendly with booze, and there were girls and girls. Life was a party with everyone invited. He married the prettiest one. You should see her now. Karen was crying. I reached out a hand, but of course, I couldn't touch her. She's a big girl, seeming bigger since I am so small. Her size made her clumsy. She used to knock things over and that made the two Savages howl.

I wasn't sure of the body's position. My memory of having had one made me feel I did. Time doesn't flow, it stutters—a minute, another. An hour, another.

Arlie came—she is like me, small and quick. She was always too quick and nervous, but I heard her more clearly than I did Karen. "What do we tell them? They're all waiting down at the bank—the cake, the decorations—the presentation—what can we do?"

I assumed this was shock. The two of them simply stood and looked at me. No tears. The scene wasn't real to them, but it is, and soon reality will give its shattering noise like the cannon they used to set off on July 4. The paramedics came. There was a long drawing, like pulling a tooth, but without the pain, as they extricated me from the car, from my body.

That body they handled with the greatest care, because family were present. It seemed humorous to me, standing there while the costumed corpse was put in the back of the ambulance. For a moment Tim Valken worried about it being a crime scene. When he said "crime scene" I started to laugh. I have—had—an unpleasant laugh, so I seldom used it. I turned it up, soundlessly, on their scene, full out, as I hadn't done in years.

Sheriff Tim was the one who surprised me most. He seemed sad. He murmured, "Great lady," to Karen and Arlie, for whom I guess I wasn't yet dead. His pain seemed real. Then he breathed in and made a leap Nureyev would die for. "It must have been something incurable—cancer, maybe, and the suffering…"

I was moved, amazed. If this is what they'll think, Karen and Mark, and their kids; Arlie and Gary, and their kids; any shame, any blame, will evaporate, at least until… until… they know that I had to do my suicide, and that the suicide couldn't have waited a day longer. Some day, I hope they'll understand. Things have gone on too long.

It's Sunday. The coroner won't come all the way from Aureole. I'm a violent death and this is a crime scene, but they won't leave me sitting or lying here until Monday afternoon, and they won't do an autopsy, in spite of what the sheriff has just proposed for me. No one will stare at my healthy heart and lungs and search for growths in my brain. No one will go into that brain and find the rage that's there, that has been there, resting now and then, but never sleeping. Let's get on with it.

Everything seemed to be taking a long time, but in the clumsy acts of getting me out of the car—the paramedics had come with a board—something had shaken loose. I could disengage. Slowly, one muscle at a time, I lifted away, free. Oh, my God! I had forgotten how age had weighed me, bones brittle and fearful, muscles trembling, flesh slack. If I had the organs that would permit me to shout, I could do it for an hour without sobbing for breath.

Could I leave? I found I could. I wanted to go down to the bank and watch them get the news. I wanted to enjoy the secret subtle signs of relief on certain faces. I've been working at that damn bank since I was twenty. Over the years I'd become an institution, and like all institutions, there are parts better not seen.

May afternoon, Sunday. It was about four p.m. by the sun, whose warmth I could no longer feel. I went to church every week for fifty-five years and I never believed a word they said. I didn't know how long I would last in this state. I didn't think that the heaven the church postulates would exist for me. All those pastors past. None of them knew. I wanted to drift down the street. It was easy in the frictionless world I now inhabited. I wanted to watch the shock hit them all and I wanted to see the faces, the dissembling, the surprise's excitement swallowed whole and sticking in the throat, "appropriate" expressions put on the faces of my co-workers, Luther assuming command, his missus—who never liked me—trying on her sorry #3—the Just Enough, careful not to betray any relief.

"What will we do with the cake and all this punch?" That would be Judy Gilner, ever practical. The garden club women would be there, too. I've led all their efforts to beautify this town, an effort that grew out of my shame and rage. It does make a person laugh.

TWO
KAREN

I STOOD THERE LIKE A fool while Tim Valken and the emergency people got Mom out of the car. I'd turned the ignition off but I didn't remember doing it. I tried to think. Mom didn't know about the surprise retirement party. I still couldn't think, or even feel much except a sick, shocky weakness, unreality making me stupid and unable to answer questions.

Tim asked the questions. Someone went for Mark and for Arlie while I stood like a sculpture of myself until Tim took me by the arm and led me inside the house. I seemed not to recognize the room or the furniture in it. Why wasn't I crying? I felt utterly stupid and utterly revealed. Why had Mom been lying dead in the car we had bought her, in the garage Mark and Gary had built for her? After I had turned off the car, why hadn't I run next door to the Prinzes', or back into the house to call for help right away? I'd pulled down the dress that had rucked up a little, showing her slip. I'd straightened her hat and put her hands in her lap. All the time I was doing those stupid things, I was murmuring: "You shouldn't be driving to the party. I was supposed to pick you up." We had planned the deception for weeks: that Arlie and I were setting up a picture-taking session for next year's Christmas cards. "What are you doing here?"

I heard Tim Valken say that Mom must have had some illness, some sensible, considerate reason for doing what she did. I knew that must be true, but I had the thought—one that keeps trying to break into my mind's conversations—that Mom wouldn't do a thing like that even for a reason like that. Mom was closed, reserved, dignified, but she never would have left us without a note, a message of some kind. There would have been something written on the stationery I gave her last year or slipped in under the edge of the figurine beside her bed, the one the kids gave her for Christmas. Maybe the secret was that she was sick after all and didn't want us to see her deformed or needing intimate care. She was always terribly conscious of how she dressed and looked. Women open their doors and get their mail in the morning wearing pajamas or bathrobes. I do that myself. Mom never did. Even for gardening there was a special outfit a little better than I would wear if I gardened, her hair just so. A disfiguring disease would—might have overwhelmed her love for us.

Mark came and brought Arlie. Mark told Sheriff Valken that he wanted to stay with me. Arlie said she would go back with a deputy to the party and get Gary and then tell everyone to go home, that Mom had become very ill suddenly and that further news would come when we knew more.

The paramedics had taken Mom's body away and there were some people in the garage now. We were in the house. I hadn't remembered going in. In the living room, Mark and I were sitting very still for what felt like hours. Mark was watchful, a comfort, being there, expecting nothing. Now and then we would be conscious of some sound or other, the house slowly shifting its old bones, appliances taking up their work or stopping it. What would we do with the food in her refrigerator? Who would come in to guard the house, now that no one lived here? Were there clothes on the line, or in the hamper ready to be washed, or in the basket ready to be folded? We'd gotten her a dryer, Arlie and I, for a long-ago birthday, but she never used it. She said she liked hanging clothes out, and the sun and the wind in them. Was there dry-cleaning waiting?

I told Mark, "Mom would never have let herself die with any kind of pain that would tear at us, any deformity. She must have had a diagnosis of something awful."

"She wouldn't have told us," Mark said. "Your mom was always dignified and reserved in her way. I've never met a woman so…I'd call her composed. Do you remember when that heavy spring snow—five, six years ago—sat so high on her roof that it didn't slide off, but pushed down hard and shattered the bedroom windows? The insurance man told me he had never seen anyone so—what did he say—unflappable. She had all the figures and measurements before the insurance people got there. They made their own, of course, but here was a woman with window glass blown all over her, over the floor in her bedroom where she was lying asleep. Shards had hit the opposite wall like knives, scarring the furniture. Slivers were all over her carpet and the bed and her body, and in her hair. She had to get up breath by breath and sift the bits of it out of her hair and from her face so very carefully, and get to a sitting position, and throw the blankets back and then gently lift them and shake them out and then throw them to the floor. I don't know if I could do that. I don't think I could be so completely patient while covered with broken glass."

I'd forgotten the event but Mark's description of her brought it back to me. Her nightgown sleeves had been shredded and she must have had glass cuts all over her upper body—I know there were some on her face, but she waved the injuries away, saying that they were minor and not even serious enough to keep her from work that morning. It must have taken her an hour, sitting up, using the bedclothes to wrap up in, cleaning out her slippers to navigate the floor. We found out that in the morning, having called the insurance company, she had dressed—and out she'd gone to the bank. There were scratches on her face, and a gash on her arm and several on her scalp.

Mom was stubborn, too. She never missed work. It was a record, a point of pride. No sick days, no vacation time, except for the federal holidays that closed the banks. People assumed that was because she had no other life than the bank, the church, and the garden club. I knew it was a gritty pride and…Mom had never been to college. She'd gotten her training as an accountant by correspondence, back when there were no computers or recognition of courses like that as being equal to a college degree. I think there was always a little fear that someone would fault her, catch an error and call her unqualified.

She'd put alum on the cuts on her scalp, bound up the arm, and gone to work, and she didn't go to the doctor until that afternoon.

"Your mom was very careful about being understood," Mark said. "There may be a note, a letter. She obviously thought this out, planned it when she got her diagnosis. She'd want to say goodbye. You may find it all in the attic in that box up there. She showed it to me once, and told me it had all her papers."

"We should go up and see, but not now," I said. "I'm not ready."

"Don't worry, there's plenty of time."

"If only she'd told us."

Mark took my hand. "That's what I'm saying. She had, in her own way, no arguments about treatment. She didn't want us spending everything we have on useless attempts to save her."

We'd been sitting side by side, shoulders touching, but not looking at each other.

"It wasn't in her to tell you such things. People who saw her in the garden, or sitting in church or at the bank, might have thought she was pleasant, that tiny, neat, quiet person, but she must have had an iron spine to raise you two alone. She never said anything about those years to me. I guess I'm saying that her silence—I mean what she did—was in character for her. There must have been a biopsy, a hard verdict. She took it by herself and made a decision."

"I don't think she understood how hard it would be for us—no hint, no last words to me or to Arlie."

While we were talking, Arlie came into the room with Gary, who looked as though he had been in a tornado, picked up and dumped somewhere. We knew he loved Mom as much as we did. I never went deeply into his past, but I knew he'd been abandoned as a child and had grown up among people who didn't give him much room for laughter or ideas. When Arlie had first brought him to dinner and we asked him what he thought about something, I forget what, he sat there stunned. It was Mom who drew him out, gently, slowly, and with her good smile. Arlie had begun to cry a little and I could see that Gary had been crying, too.

By the time the people examining the scene had left the garage and Mom's body had been taken away to the funeral home in Aureole, we were sitting in near darkness. We knew we should go back down the hill and see to the kids and let them know, and comfort them. Jenny would be relentless, asking, probing. I couldn't stand that right now. She was thirteen and full of herself. Mike and Evan would follow with questions, too. Put my kids and Arlie's together and there would be too much to handle.

I got up and went to the window. In the soft night, the moon was competing with a glow from downtown. "I think we should go home," I said.

Arlie got up, Gary and Mark came over and hugged us, and then I hugged both of them and we left. I was glad to let Mark drive us to Barb's house to pick up our two. I don't think I could have directed us to that house, although I had known Barb for years. I don't think I could have told where *our* house was at that moment.

The kids must have known that something was up. The party at the bank had been dampened by their grandmother's absence, the message being that she had been taken ill suddenly. People had continued to chat and the cake was brought out.

People had drifted off and Barb had taken all of them to her house, where they watched TV and played a video game, but they must have been feeling the vibe of upset and trembling around them.

I wanted the kids at home with Mark and me, just the four of us. I don't know why. My mood was visceral, overwhelming, unexplainable, like what Mom had done.

THREE
LILY

I BEGAN TO WONDER WHAT my possibilities were, now that I was body-less. When I disengaged I found that I could slide on the air, float or flow. I thought I might do what Dracula does in the movies, sifting through keyholes or under doors. I found it could be done but that it was painful. I still had the metaphor of body, of feeling, pain and pleasure, of vision, hearing, and touch. What I experienced in this state was like the weightlessness of a carnival ride. I would enter and exit rooms and buildings in the normal way.

Learning how to flow, I let the afternoon downhill air currents carry me to Main Street and the bank. I hadn't wanted this party. My retirement was mandatory. I was officially sixty-eight, and everyone knew it. At least there would be no speeches from Luther.

Using my shoulders and feet the way a swimmer would, I flowed in when Ethel Yost slipped out for a smoke. The reality was almost as comic as my fantasy had been. Secretaries were crying; Luther, who had been our president for only two years, was acting as though he'd lost his only friend, but I could see relief leaking out like wisps of down from a pillow's stretched seam. Because they hadn't heard how I had died, their shock was unmediated by disapproval. The whole scene was as gratifying as a knife in the heart of an enemy.

I had kept my level of caution high, knowing how people who listen in from hiding rarely hear good things spoken about themselves. Perhaps the public nature of all of this kept the hard words back behind the tongue, but I loved what I saw. Fake sorrow over a fake loss. I began to laugh. I almost never laughed in life. A little smile was all they got. Now, I was free to hate and to enjoy my revenge. I lay on the floor and laughed and laughed, the sound echoing in my head and nowhere else.

Everyone got stuffed with cake and punch, and Marcie Durage got sat on for mentioning that reconfiguring my office space would allow more room for the new equipment. Marcie was always tactful as a rock through a picture window. Mary Anne McGuire's eyeliner and mascara ran down her cheeks, giving her the look of a work of modern art. Her mother used to give herself to anyone who asked. Her brother was one of those football hero mouth-breathers, ten kinds of sex, never in a bed.

Now that I was downtown and not quite walking, not having to pant with exertion or feel pain in my knees, I decided to visit what was left of some of the places where I had grown up. There was little enough there. The bank, of course, was in its place, though tarted up with a new façade. The school we all went to was gone, its place taken by the hygienic-looking learning factory that Karen and Arlie attended. Henderson's Market, where my parents worked, is gone—no one shops in town anymore. It's been left to boutiques and tourist stuff. The real shopping is now out at the mall.

I drifted down the older streets, past Lowayne's house. I hadn't seen her at the party. I assumed she was there but left early, maybe even before the announcement. People in the room would have walked past her, verifying their opinion of her by noting the double rotting-fruit smell of gin and diabetes. She was an Ellie, so old people might nod to her. She was at home now. I could have looked in, but why? Drunk and dull. I went on up the street, noting the budding trees on Prospector, then floated down Third to Larissa's, the Bendixen house, still here, but latticed and gentrified into a neo-pseudo-steamboat Gothic confection. Larissa had sold it after Doc and

Anne died and she and Richard now lived up near the
ski area in the new development.

Upscale. We have gone upscale. The new money
people took over and went Decorator in the places
where the river runs through town, so nothing remains
of the geography of that part of my life. I was behind the
gentrification and busy to stamp out poverty and shame.
It's been planted with trees, and I talked the garden
club into getting its community-minded fingers on it,
and I got the chamber of commerce to put plaques on a
memorial statue of a miner who looks with bronze eyes
on the joggers running for their health. Those joggers all
look like Death is after them on a skateboard.

There will be a funeral. I have no interest in seeing
my body or witnessing any of the things done to it to
make it fit for viewing. No doubt Pastor Fearing will
conduct the service. If he knew anything about me and
my reasons, he would make an example of me, telling
the mourners that my causes of anger should disappear
the way the bones of my parents have. I can hear him
now—"forgive." He's not smart enough to know what
that would mean. He slathers forgiveness like store icing
on a cupcake, the icing being cheaper to produce than
the cake. He wouldn't know what I was talking about.
Now I wonder who would. Lowayne would, now.

By the time I got back, the party was long over and the bank closed. I decided to return there bright and early, as I had done for all these years, well dressed, head high, underpaid.

There is no sleeping in this state, but there is a sort of easing. This moment should have been one of those that we look forward to and remember with smiles—a May evening in the Ute Valley, for heaven's sake—a glorious place in the peak of the year. I drifted away from town, away from the changes and the new developments grown up by the river, and sought out the little loop on its far side where its course had once run. There was a little pocket of unclaimed ground. Aspen in a stand were giving birth to themselves, bursting the tiny brown protective pods that hold the secret of their limitations. At their bases, leaves of past years lay restless under the fingers of the light breeze. A little farther up was the graveyard, set on the slight rise the river had left. Over the years, willow shrubs and aspen had made themselves comfortable there and held the land. There was no gold here, and it was left to be a burial place. I thought to go up there, but I didn't want to meet any other ghosts, if some still remained. I would hate to encounter Addie and Harmon, those two old gorgons, or the dozen or so witnesses.

But I was curious. I might see them before they saw me, and there was one person there I would like to see again: Dr. Bendixen, Larissa's father, whom I'd mourned longer than she had. I pulled my body out long in the river and left near the road that led up to the graveyard.

There were no ghosts there, only old snow and new grass that announced itself where it had drawn away. I rested there, lying between the gravestones, and counted the stars that the glow of light from Gold Flume and Callan allowed us.

FOUR
LOWAYNE

WHEN I WAS FIFTY AND alcoholic and gone through all the programs and promises and the hundred times trying, I quit sobriety and settled for what I wanted, and it worked. I drank less, just a constant little buzz and a comfort, knowing that I always had a supply, a bottle, whenever I needed a belt. Because of that, a fear that I would run out no longer ruled my life. I was free to think about other things.

One of the things I can't afford no more is vanity. Another is what other people think of me. Charlie and me sure done enough when he was alive and we was drinking in the old way against ourselves to ruin any reputation we could have had. I thought I was armed pretty good against the outside world, but when Lily died, it made me remember lots of the things time and booze blotted out.

God, they was poor. Lily come in town to school every day with her folks, retards, both of them, who worked at Henderson's. They done all the fetch-and-carry at the store, but they couldn't fill orders except if it was one or two things and then you'd have to say each thing one at a time and then they'd go get it. Missus was smart enough to know she was dumb; I don't think Mister was. One thing we all knew and that was that they was scared, both of them. Holly Williams—I haven't thought of that guy in years—he said they had escaped from some kind of retard asylum and was afraid of being put back there, so they lived quiet as death in that squatters' shack a quarter of a mile up the Hungry Mother and worked hard as they could, and you could see them hanging on to each other when they left work to go home.

We was the Ellies, names all started with L. That was in third grade when the teacher noticed that and pointed it out. I realize now, thinking about it, that Lily's folks didn't have to pay for food or rent—they got the throwaways and dented cans from work, stale bread, vegetables and fruit no one would buy. Any money went on clothes for Lily. She was always clean and dressed. Mrs. Henderson sent to Sears for clothes for them all— enough to keep them decent, if unironed. Lily came to school with her folks and then after school she went to Henderson's to wait for them to go home together, but after she got to be an Ellie, she would go to Larissa's or our house or to LuAnne's. She would wait there for her folks to get through cleaning up after the store closed. If we hadn't been Ellies I don't think we would have been friends—funny when you think of it. Larissa, she was the stand-out, beautiful, too. Lily was small and had long, dark hair, straight. I was big and had hair like one of them curly sheep, nothin' blonde then, gray now. Larissa's folks was rich in the way we thought of as rich then. He was Dr. Bendixen, *the* doc in town and a good man, one of them good people sprinkled around here and there to leaven the world. Mrs. B was a little like they say, eager socially, but good. LuAnne, she was twelve, she died, and everyone was surprised but me. She got polio the year that kids in Callan and Bluebank got it. There was something soft about her, sweet, like Beth in *Little Women* that they made us read in school, who you knew was going to die, anyway. Her folks was quiet, but not like the Higginses, Lily's people, who were quiet being scared—it was like they didn't want to take up too much room or breathe too much air. If they was alive today, they would fit right in, don't leave no footprint.

Then there was me. I liked to have fun. I should have been a boy. I think I would have made a good one, climbing, not caring if I fell. Fighting would have been okay, too. I wanted to fly. I was the first girl around here to drive a car. I let Bobby Valken do things to me so he would let me drive his car and when I met Charlie, when I was sixteen, I saw someone just like me, loving fun.

Lily—Lily was quiet out of need. I don't think she was ashamed of her folks; I think she was scared for them. Did she know they was runaways? They was delicate some way. They knew they could be fired, just like that, and then no one would want to give them work. They could say or do something that would make people angry. People did laugh at them some, but laughing is okay as long as it don't turn ugly.

Two things happened when we was twelve. One, LuAnne died, and two, Lily's folks died. When that happened it was a Sunday in November so they was home up there on the Hungry Mother and snow, a soft flutter of it way up on that mountain, slid and then slid again and gathered more and more, harder, icier snow that pulled and took the whole front face off that mountain. It was the biggest avalanche anyone had ever seen and it grew, pulling everything along with it, including them two in their house. Lily was at Sunday school because Mrs. Henderson had made a project out of her. After Sunday school Lily went to our house for the afternoon. We was playing when Doc come up the walk and knocked at our door and talked with my folks and then got her and I guess told her she couldn't go home. The avalanche had blocked the road two hundred yards wide and thirty feet deep. It didn't take an Einstein to know there was no way in hell those folks could have avoided what happened. Doc took her into town to the Reeds. LuAnne had died and with the war just over, the government was too busy to stick their noses in and whip Lily off to an orphanage, so the Reeds give her a home. We all thought that was a good idea—she could stay with us in school, be where she knew everybody, and be an Ellie. I think there was a little jolt about the clothes—Lily wearing LuAnne's dresses. It must have soured her some. LuAnne was normal size. Lily was kind of pinched, small, flat; they swam on her even though they might have been two or three years outgrown.

Living with the Reeds was like living in a cotton ball, soft but muzzled. Lily didn't know much about how normal people did things—setting a table, eating, washing, ironing. She was always clean. The Higginses was very clean, but I think they done it with washrags out of a bucket and Lily had to learn how to use soap and toothbrush and all that.

The Reeds wasn't happy with Lily—I got this from her, not from them. Every Sunday, they would show up with her at church. They came to her events, plays, and her graduation from grade school, but seeing them together I got the feeling you get when you meet someone on a narrow street and for three seconds the two of you dance right to left and left to right, smiling to hide your impatience—put off, not natural.

I know they didn't want Lily working in the bakery. The Molinos come the first year of the war and set up, and Town took to them like they was born here. Most women made their own cookies, ordinary cake or pie, bread. *They* made special cakes with letters on the frosting; rolls, too. Nobody else made rolls. When she was thirteen, Lily got a job there, afternoons and Saturday, and she paid the Reeds. She said it helped. I didn't know why, then. Now I think it made them and everybody know that she was a boarder, not a daughter, and that everybody could relax and not try for something they wasn't going to get.

At fourteen, we went to high school, leaving Gold Flume on a bus all the way to the Consolidated in Aureole. Only a few of the kids went all the way through to graduation. I didn't and neither did Lily, and it annoyed the Reeds. She started to work at the bakery full time. I got work at the mine in Bluebank, checking men in and out and answering letters and doing ordinary secretarial things. That's when I met Charlie and we was married, when I was sixteen. That was so long ago. When I think about it, it gives me the creeps. I know there'll be a funeral for Lily at church. I guess I'll have to go. I'll sit in the back. The last time I was in church was for Charlie's funeral twenty years ago. We was a ski town by then, but without these big fancy houses they got now.

We was the Ellies since we was in third grade, but by the time we was seventeen, we knew we wasn't close—not going to be close for life. I was married to Charlie and he wanted people to party with, and Lily was mousy and quiet and when she wasn't at the bakery, she was at the Reeds' helping Mrs. Reed or up in LuAnne's room reading. I think she missed going to school. Larissa, Doc's daughter, was gentry in town, getting ready for college, certainly not ready to laugh it up with Charlie and me. Sometimes we'd get together at town functions, Memorial Day, or Fourth of July, and talk about what we was doing. Town saw us together and assumed we was still as close as we was as kids.

We don't do Memorial Day no more. I liked what we did—Town going up to their dead in the cemetery and weeding and pruning and maybe propping up a stone that was fallen over. Later there was picnics, kids moving from one to another in the May weather. They got a man there now is supposed to do all that, the care of it.

When we got to be eighteen, Charlie got work in Bluebank and I got pregnant and Larissa went away to college, and Lily met Del Beausoleil that some Korean should have shot in the war.

FIVE
LUTHER HAYES

I SUPPOSE IT HAPPENS ALL the time—juniors who know more than their superiors, leaders, commanders. It happened to me first in Viet Nam—maybe that's the source of my problem here—the damn woman knew this town like a priest knows Mass, sing it, say it—she knew all the Valley towns and who'd just come and whose people had ventured over the pass in 1873 in a covered wagon. I was a captain fighting the good fight in Tokyo and Fussa, and one day found myself deployed In-Country with a group of the scrapings of other units. My sergeant was Winger, whom the men respected a hell of a lot more than they respected me. He was smart, and better yet, he was battle smart in everything from how to wear socks to how to talk down a fear-paralyzed buddy. He was tactful in telling me things, but after a while, his expertise began to rankle. He had two pet peeves: pot and dirt.

Everyone in Fussa smoked pot. It eased boredom and mellowed a man as booze didn't often do. There were fewer fights in the barracks when the cloud rose over the cots.

My first brush with Winger came In-Country when I saw men smoking and I walked on by. He gently reminded me that weed was illegal and against military discipline and regulations. I was cavalier, not wanting to be seen as puritanical. "Why not a little pot to mellow a man out, Sergeant?"

"Sir, mellow is the last thing you want in a combat zone, sir. Mellow is stupid and fearless and fearless and stupid is dead. Crowley and Bain, who died before you got here, were fearless and friendly as puppy dogs on pot, standing up in the paddies because it was unpleasant to lie with a face in the mud when people were shooting. Dead. Two others were incautious, not looking, and set off mines they should have seen. Louis got snakebite because he tried to befriend the snake when he was in a mellow mood."

In a country where shoes went rancid and everything rotted and stank, he was demanding, and there were always those tactful suggestions about where to bed down and where not, and how to keep clean and how to eat and how to look and what to look for. Winger saved us many times, but in the end, even the tact became humiliating and his "Capt'n Hayes, sir…" a thumb on a sore.

So when I came here and met the local example, something grated, even after all those years, and even before I was fully aware of why I was griped. Again there was the tact, the careful suggestion, the instruction given in the form of a suggestion or a sudden idea, like the laxative hidden in the ball of fat you give to a sick dog.

And there were the saves that should have brought gratitude from me, but didn't. I was ready to okay a loan I had every reason to believe was good. It was early in my career here—I had been told, or maybe warned, by Jepson before he left that Mrs. Lily B knew everything about everybody in the Ute Valley. I told Mrs. B I was ready to recommend the loan. She looked at me and cocked her head a little—"I wouldn't." I showed her the paperwork. She said, "Have you been out to that ranch? He's got two wells, both polluted with toxic minerals, and he's got a mortgage with a bank in Wyoming. He's not a bad man, but he's the inheritor of three generations of bad luck and overreaching by his father. He also has family responsibilities that keep him from putting his mind on his situation. I'd let this one go."

She said it all reasonably. We denied the loan, and three months later the land was sold off and the family gone. There's a trailer park there now and they had to go to three hundred eighty feet to get clean water.

There were many other times, too. Some we would have turned down that she said were good and should go through, and which turned out to be solid and got us accounts that we would not have had, good accounts.

I was grateful—I'm not a fool or a madman, but in Viet Nam after a while, there was a feeling that, saved or not, Winger had humiliated me. In my own mind, Lily Beausoleil did the same. She was discreet to a fault, but there was that look in her eyes—and then a grimace, a gesture—and I started to have dreams about her. There was one where she sent me on a secret mission in a war, and I couldn't find the place where I was supposed to meet my squad. I had neglected to find out where the place was and had no way of tracing it. I woke sweating and trembling.

So at the retirement party—the secretaries had gotten that up—I was all ready to parade her virtues in an introduction I had sweated over, to Betty's caustic comments. Betty had never liked our bookkeeper-accountant—something about a tiff they had had when we first came. She got to the party under duress and in an extremely sour mood. We waited. Two p.m. came and went. Some of the old-timers had started their reminiscences and were happy enough, but outside the church social hall the sky was that shimmering blue that is, I think, unique to this part of the world. I wanted to be outside, on our patio, with a game on the radio, lying in a lounge chair with a beer or two in the cooler close at hand. I was just thinking of how I might get away after my speech before they broke out the cake and punch when one of the daughters and a deputy came in to give us the news of Lily's sudden illness. Flight was impossible, then. People were asking each other questions that no one could answer. I caught Betty's eye and she gave me that quick smile, then put her concern on in a flash. Women really are savages.

People were talking about a fall, a broken hip. We stayed for fifteen minutes, Betty and I, after they brought out the cake and I gave my little speech, modifying it to fit the new situation. We ducked out after that and went home, but by the time I got the lounge chair up from the basement and set it up and got the beers and the cooler, it was too chilly to be outside. Damn the woman! We only found out later—Betty got the call—that Mrs. B was dead.

I know I learned things from her, and from Winger, about leadership—dedication, really. Both were intense and fully dedicated. I don't think Mrs. B took a single day off except when the bank was closed. Winger was more important in the war than I was, and Lily Beausoleil was more important at the bank. If I don't admit that to anyone else, I'll have to face it to myself. My feeling, if I'm honest? Relief.

SIX
KAREN

WE FELT LIKE INVALIDS, ARLIE and I, sitting at the kitchen table in Mom's house, waiting for the day to move over us. Mark, Gary, and Pastor Fearing were in the living room, making funeral plans. We had called some people, and they had taken over that job when they saw we had had enough. Now, with no jobs to do, we sat in the enforced idleness of shock, incompetent and restless. I thought to ask Arlie what her earliest memories of Mom were. She's two years younger than I am and now and then I've been surprised by the differences in our memories.

She heard my question and sat for a while, until I thought she didn't want to say anything. Then she said, "When Mom tore down the drapes in the library and living room—they were so dusty and faded—do you remember? I guess I never realized how she must have hated them, and the darkness there. She had such a look on her face—anger, or just a stubborn will—a need. She was standing a little to the side, pulling all of them down, and they came, rods and all and a big cloud of dust and then, how the light came in, streaming, dust-motes riding on the shaft. The windows were dirty, but even so, the room was changed; the whole house lightened, and went easy."

"That was because Harmon and Addie—remember having to call them Mr. and Mrs. Beausoleil, never Grandma or Grandpa?—were gone and we had the house, ours for the first time, and not having to rush all the time and run to the bells they rang. Fix my pillow. Pick up that book."

"I guess I don't remember—I have only a hazy picture of them."

I was amazed at that. The pair of them had loomed in my life, and I know they did in Mom's. There were bells that summoned Mom and us to fetch, to carry, to bring up clothes and dinner trays, to take out things they'd finished or that displeased them. I never saw Mrs. do a single woman thing: smoothing, folding, carrying, washing, wringing, polishing, replacing, supplying, walking with things in her hands. And he was usually in the library among his books, always querulous and demanding. Had a pen been moved? Had a book not been dusted? "Did you know that Mom read some of those books before the old man died? I don't think he ever found out that she was taking them and putting them back before he noticed."

"I never knew that." Arlie was shaking her head. "To me it was only that something dark and smelly and angry had gone and that—light came, and laughter, cookies, Mom's face happy. Then there were the flowers."

"The flowers came later," I told her, amazed at the difference two years makes. Mr. and Mrs. were real presences in my life and their scorn for Mom was as obvious and constant as the pain of a twisted arm, that feeling of hot-and-cold together. "He called me clumsy. I was big, even then, big-hipped, big-handed, and they said I couldn't be their boy's because he was dark and well made, like Mom, only not quick like Mom. We all had bony noses, where theirs were flatter and wider. Mr. Beausoleil—Harmon to you, went first. Do you remember some kind of cough?"

"Oh, God, yes—I remember the coughs."

"They came like waves with a drawing back and a gasp and again and again."

"I don't remember anything about her actual death, or the funeral. There's that big stone up at the graveyard, but I don't remember getting there, or how much we were involved in the ceremonies."

"He got worse—Harmon. The bell was constant by then. I had the feeling he could walk, but didn't want to—I don't remember if Mom was working at the bank by then, but I think she was. People came in—I remember that—to help. My memory is that he argued that Mom should be doing it all herself, all the work of laundry, cooking, and us, all in that big house, upstairs-downstairs a dozen times a day."

"Then they both were gone and we all took a breath, a deep breath through that filthy window that screamed when we tried to open it, not having been cracked in fifty years. We pulled air in, even though it was winter air, feeling free."

I had a sudden idea. "Let's go up to the attic and get Mom's memory box and go through it."

Arlie surprised me. "I don't know if I'm ready." She looked around wanly and then nodded. "Yes, okay, we'd better do it now. We'll have to go back to work in a day or so, and there'll be all this to do, her clothes and the kitchen things, and all the stuff we and the kids gave her over the years, and the furniture. I remember the new things, piece by piece, years in between."

We went up the stairs, the uncarpeted ones at the end of the hall on the second floor, our steps loud as we went. There, too, was a spareness and order. The big attic room was all but empty; extra furniture from Harmon and Addie's time had been taken away along with all the clothing they had piled away up there, for use God only knew when. I remember our doing that years ago, packing all the dead-smelling, unwashed blouses and thick long skirts fifty years out of date even then, and bringing working men up there to take the chairs and the extra bedstead and the boxes we filled down and away.

Mom had a large footlocker, something our father must have brought home from Korea. It was metal and painted that khaki green you see on trucks and jeeps. Its lock had been broken years ago. There was the smell of attics everywhere, the combination of wood heated and cooled again and again for a hundred years, worn clothing, the greasy smell of moths and the sweetish-acidic smell of mouse urine; the smell of printed paper, the after-tang rancid oil—cedar or lavender—with the things the old lady had stored away.

Even in someone you've known all your life, there's mystery. Mom's life had been Spartan-simple: us, her garden club, church, the bank. We thought we knew or had seen all the things that had gone into the locker. The evidence would all be here, our pictures, prize essays, anything written or printed about us, birth certificates, all in special folders in the trunk. In its folder would be the deed to the house, receipted bills, income-tax materials saved for years. We knew there would be no stock or bond certificates. She once said to me that working at a bank had made her witness to financial frailty in all its forms."

So we opened the footlocker with no special excitement and took the boxes from it. Each was labeled in her careful, legible hand. The sight of her writing brought tears. There were all its unique features: the backward slant of the *D*s like the stop signal of a policeman against the forward push of her other letters, the single stroke of her *L*s and the elongated *P*. It was Mom. I started to cry in earnest.

Arlie let me go for a minute or two and then said, "I feel like I'm stifling. Can't we open a window?" Arlie is small and dark, bigger than Mom, of course, but she gets short of breath. Luckily, there was a window. I had to beat on it to release it from its over-painted casements. When I got back, Arlie had all the boxes out and was going through the familiar one of our early lives.

There were pictures of us and our friends, in fashions we had thought we looked good in at that time, report cards from grade school, our old autograph books, school magazines, patiently fading, and newspaper clippings yellowing as we lived past them, graduation certificates, elementary school, high school, college.

We went through the box with the tax returns, the notarized this and that, a life shown in bills and notifications and certificates, two summonses to jury duty. I had forgotten those times she had spent in Aureole at the courthouse.

There was another box, smaller, marked *Private*, and what could be in that one? We pulled up the lid and saw Mom's own certificates, and there were letters and pictures and articles about the garden club, obituaries of two or three people, and a long article on yellowing paper about Larissa's father, Dr. Bendixen.

The pictures weren't organized. New, old were all random in the box, unlike the careful treatment of the other boxes. We separated them from the letters and articles we planned to read later. We spread the pictures out on the floor and then began to slide them into a rough order, by year. Some of them were marked on the back in Mom's careful script.

The recent ones were mostly of Mom's garden club arrangements. What struck Arlie, who pointed it out to me, was that they were almost all without people. Here and there, someone would be holding a bouquet, perhaps, or posed with a flowering bush. Mom was very seldom shown.

We began to go back—there were Larissa and Lowayne standing in various poses, their school graduation with other friends, Larisssa's wedding picture,

Lowayne's. There were the Ellies, Larissa full face and obviously presenting herself. Lowayne—God, what a pretty girl she had been, a big smile, bright eyes, a lovely figure. She and Larissa were in lightly patterned summer dresses. They must have been sixteen or so. Mom was there, but not full face. She was looking at Larissa and Lowayne and she was in a white blouse and dark skirt, too serious, almost formal against the patterns of the light batiste or voile dresses of the other two. Mom stood straight, very small, dark, and with the flatness in the face poor people have—old-time ones, who were undernourished all their growing years.

There were Larissa, Lowayne, and LuAnne, so the picture must have been taken before LuAnne's death at twelve, but they looked younger. Larissa was, as usual, the focus of the group, Lowayne and LuAnne standing at her sides, and in the back, behind them and barely seen, Mom.

In none of the other pictures was Mom present at all. There were ten pictures of Del Beausoleil, our father. We had never seen these pictures and were greedy, all but arguing—"Let me see that one"—even as we had another picture in our hands. "Wait—let's get them in order." Arlie sighed and we bit our lips and lay them all out like cards in a game: three rows of three. The first was a soldier in a village—it must have been in Korea.

Can a person swagger standing still? He is bare-chested and stands crinkle-eyed with the sun, but with a boyish grin and a very handsome face. Around him in the background are other soldiers, mostly bare-chested, too, and in summer gear. He stands completely at ease, weight on one foot, in the American slouch. The photo has obviously been much handled—its edges are worn and there is a fold line on the lower left edge—but Delbert Harmon Beausoleil is very much in his element, belonging.

First row: at home—three of these, taken on the same day, in various poses, still wearing some of his Army issue. In one, obviously commanded by his mother, he stands holding an open display box with his patches, medals, and campaign ribbons. He looks pained. In one he clowns. The third catches him not posing. Someone must have called out to him from out of the picture because he looks up, expectantly. He is, in all, boyish and boyishly handsome with fine white teeth that show in a delighted, radiant smile, proud-shy. "And those eyes…" Arlie murmured. The color pictures show the dark hair, tanned face, and eyes the color of blue topaz, radiantly blue.

There are the later ones, three with locals, friends at recognizable places in town, one or two of which are still here. There's one in a hard hat and he looks older. We put that one alone, at the bottom.

Two are heartbreaking, but only for those who know the couple. In one, he is standing behind a girl, holding her by the shoulders. It's Mom, a skinny, agonizingly shy Mom in that white blouse and dark skirt. She faces the camera like a woman in a police shot. At the same session, Del is talking to a friend and the girl is looking at him. The picture is unposed. She is half-dead with love. Her face is illuminated with it. He is unaware, in the middle of his talk with the friend, one hand up in a gesture underscoring the point he is making.

There were no more photographs, but there were articles with grainy shots, one of a graduation class, high school, showing Del, middle row, third from the left. One article was about returning vets, in the local paper. Del was not among them, but his was among the names of the local boys who served.

A big surprise. There was a two-sheet news article, folded and put in a cardboard folder: *LOCAL MAN SAVES FELLOW WORKER*. The story described an accident where an earthmover had run into the edge of a large boulder buried at a dig site. The huge piece of equipment had begun to fall over. The driver had been thrown out of the cab and would have been crushed under the falling machine had not Delbert "Del" Beausoleil, who was standing nearby, run to the fallen man and pulled him away as the earthmover canted over and then fell.

The picture with the article had been dark when taken. Now it was all but black. There was to be a reward given by the company. So Delbert Beausoleil, our father, was a hero, a medalled warrior who had seen action and who knew how much there was of pain and danger in a distant and treacherous place. He had brought his heroism home to save still another life. Heroes are modest, and because they are, are often unsung. We shivered, Arlie and I, with pleasure. Our father had been looking for work, for a new start in a place where there were more possibilities, when he died. Mom had told us that she didn't know how he died, or exactly where, because for some reason, it was a while before his identification was made. Addie and Harmon would have wanted the body returned, but that hadn't been possible and they seemed to have blamed Mom for not demanding it.

Why hadn't Mom shown us these pictures or shared the story of our father's heroism? Maybe she thought we would dwell so much on the sorrow of losing him so early in our lives that we would make a picture of him that no other man could equal.

SEVEN
GARY

EVEN NOW, IN THIS PAIN, a dragging spiritual bellyache, I see how good, how warm, it is to have a family. Mark and I are making funeral plans. Arlie and I talk, make love, comforting love, and afterward, we talk about the grief we're sharing.

I met Arlie when she had her accident. It was in Denver, close to Colorado Women's College. I'd gone to a store near there, on a job interview. She was waiting for the bus. I was there, wool gathering as usual, and not looking at any of the people next to me. The bus came and people got in. I was behind a girl. She had a purse and some packages, and books, both hands full, and when she was on the step up, the driver suddenly closed the doors and started.

The woman was trapped, one leg on the step, held by the door, and the bus was moving. Behind her, purse and packages were being slung in all directions. People were pounding on the sides of the bus to try to get the driver to stop. I picked her up and started running with her to keep up with the bus so she wouldn't be dragged, hoping the bus wouldn't gain speed too soon for me to keep up. Behind me, cars were blowing their horns, hoping to alert the driver. After a block he slowed and stopped and the door opened and the woman—young, deathly pale—fell into my arms. Some people were running after us with her possessions. She looked up at me—her coat and dress had been pulled and ripped. She smiled and said, "We've got to stop meeting like this," and fainted. That was Arlie. She was small, dark-haired, and she looked prim until she smiled and her eyes crinkled. The smile was radiant.

She was looking for work after graduation. I was working on a job I hoped to quit. She wasn't as badly hurt as I thought—the cop told me I had saved her from serious injury. I went to the hospital with her. She had a dislocated hip and two broken ribs and had been badly roughed up. They popped the hip back in place and said she should take some time off.

I wasn't quite ready to quit my job—I didn't have any other, but I wanted to keep seeing her, so I told my boss the story of what had happened, but said the girl was my sister. I asked for three days off. We came home, here, to Gold Flume, to visit.

Mark and Karen were already married and had had Jenny. My introduction to them all was at a dinner Mrs. B made at the big, old house, halfway up the hill on First Street. I was presented as a hero, toasted and cheered, but that wasn't what made me respond so deeply, set a direction, come to a place I had, without knowing it, always wanted to be. They were all at the table, eating and talking, and Mom—Mrs. Beausoleil, then—was at the head of the table, pleasantly engaged with the talk. It all felt so easy and relaxed, so open and unforced. I was seeing for the first time what a family could be, what strength and love it could impart. Now and then, Mrs. B. would add her own ideas, always moderately and with a little dry humor. She had welcomed me without any weighing or judgment about who I was or what I did. Of course, I knew that her acceptance wasn't for my own qualities, but because Arlie thought I was worthy. Her manner seemed to suggest that I would soon make my way into her good graces on my own. Sooner than I expected, this acceptance came. I began to call her Lily and then Mom.

I'd grown up at the end of the orphanage era and the beginning of the foster-care idea. The orphanage had been clean, well run, and cold as ice. The staff were pleasant and glazed as the plastic leaves on a decorator plant. Then there were the foster homes, three of them, and none of my doing wrong. In each, I was an outsider, made allowance for, but grudgingly or with a patronizing bit: "Who have we here?" "These are the rules of the house," they would say, "get along with me and I'll get along with you." It wasn't until I was in Gold Flume at the table Mom headed that I felt accepted with anything like pleasure.

Arlie and I married and Mom helped us set up in an apartment near the ski area. She had always supported herself, but there was nothing extra. She did know how to help us to get the best for the money we had.

I began to see myself through Mom's eyes. I relaxed and began to grow. I was working as a maintenance man at the ski area, the only job I could get in Gold Flume at that time. I took classes offered in Aureole in conjunction with CU and got a degree in business administration. Four years ago, I became the operations manager of the ski area.

I like the prestige of the job. I like wearing a suit sometimes and work clothes at other times. I like our house, which we built with a very friendly loan from the area management. Mom supplied contacts, but she gave me something special and irreplaceable. In her presence,

I felt rooted, solid, at home. I stopped thinking like an orphan, someone pulling on a torn and gaping robe that wouldn't quite cover his nakedness. I'm good at my job. I've gone miles beyond where I could have imagined myself and now I'm sitting with a good, kind, intelligent family mourning as one of them.

They've puzzled about how she died. People are talking suicide. That's nonsense. Mom had started the car in the garage and planned to open the doors when the car was running. She must have felt faint, or even fainted, and the gas overcame her. In those closed quarters, a one-car garage, it would have taken minutes. She was dressed to go out. Her death was an accident. That, and nothing more, and sad enough.

EIGHT
JENNY

MOM ASKED ME IF I wanted to say something at Gran's funeral. It was a big responsibility. I would be representing all the grandkids, being the oldest, but I know that we all loved Gran and that she loved us. Too, I'd be talking to all the people who came to the funeral.

I started out by writing about how her voice would be in the aspen trees that are in the graveyard. It was very beautiful and I was proud of having written it. I wrote about how her spirit would be with us, guiding us through life, and how her eyes would shine on us from heaven. I was really proud of that because it was beautiful, too. I copied it out. It said things that included a lot of poetry, how the leaves turn up so the sound is like applauding, and it was kind of applauding Gran.

The next day I read it to appreciate it one more time before I put it in the envelope to be ready for when I read it at the funeral. It really stank. I wondered how that could happen, how I could think it was so good when it was really so rotten the next day. I read it again. Yes, it stank. I went to Mom and told her what happened. She said that both she and Aunt Arlie had had the same thing happen when they were young. She said that it took them a lot longer than it had taken me to realize that fancy and billowy doesn't always mean good. I almost started to cry because I didn't know what to do. Mom said for me to tell why I loved Gran and why I would miss her.

That was a lot harder. It's hard to say what a person is like who has been around all your life and is just part of the way things are. You don't want to talk about somebody's smell or touch. You want to be more intellectual. It's important not to screw up. I made a list:

(1) She was always glad to see us.

(2) She always knew what we were into so she could talk about it.

(3) Once I had a fight with my best friend, Carla, and Gran asked me some questions that made me know what had gone wrong.

(4) She could be funny. Once, me and my cousin, Michelle, were goofing around downstairs in the church hall. Someone said for us to be quiet and reverent

because this was God's house. Gran said, "Don't worry; He doesn't come down here." It made us laugh, but we did stop clowning around. I didn't put that in because people might take it the wrong way, so I told about what happened when Evan was about six and he pulled down one of the window blinds in the living room, which Mom had to put up because the house got too hot in the summer. We all heard that tearing sound and the loud bang and came running in, and Gran went to Evan, who was crying because he was scared—the blind was really big compared to him. Gran looked at the window and said, "Shades of night are gently falling." And the grownups were laughing, so we knew it was all right.

I did say that (5) sometimes Mom and Dad were busy, but when Gran got home from the bank on the days she wasn't visiting what she called her shut-ins, we knew we could always go up to her house and she would listen when we had a gripe with our parents or our friends. I didn't do it much, but the thing is that she was there, and because I knew that, it was a big thing.

(6) Everybody in town knew Gran, so it made us feel like we were in a big, nice family.

Of course there was an argument. I wanted to wear my turquoise flared skirt to the church and my pink blouse. Mom never wanted me to get that blouse because she said it was TMI—Too Much Information—and a little too tight, and besides, it wasn't right for a funeral. What else did I have? What I wear to school, which has a dress code? We argued until I said, "You're going to ruin this whole funeral for me," and Mom started to laugh, and then I did, too.

I wrote the speech, using my list, and Mom said it was fine. Aunt Arlie had a lilac blouse she said I could wear and my school skirt and that would look okay.

NINE
LILY

THE FUNERAL WAS ALL I could have wished, hilarious, too, with a few exceptions. Pastor Fearing did not disappoint, giving his usual boilerplate Gone To A Better Place, as if he could know where the hell I had gone, and in my case not soon enough according to his dear wife, Cheryl, who sighed and shook her head with its honey-dyed curls. That woman must have a line to the police frequency, knowing about my death before anyone else so she could get to the beauty salon. Pastor was at his orotund best. There were sniffles and noses being blown throughout the packed church. Half of the weeping was allergy. It's May, after all.

Second up at bat was Melody Reimer, dying to head the garden club, telling everyone how wonderful a gardener I was, what a green thumb I had, a magical way with any growing thing. I ground my ghostly teeth at that one. Green thumb my foot! I worked very hard, I studied and devoted a great deal of time and energy to my gardening, and to that club, which I founded. Melody had the nerve to call what I did magic. I made that magic, every scrap of it, and this wasn't the first time I was annoyed when someone gave me that stupid compliment about my magic touch. They used it to escape the knowledge of their own sloth and laziness.

I was surprised, though, when she went on with what the club had decided, which I hadn't known, that there had been an emergency meeting. She said they had decided unanimously to establish the triangular plot on the river walk as the Lily Beausoleil Overlook. Slips from my own garden and some of the plants there would be taken and transplanted to that site, and a seat would be placed around the tree there. Because it was so close to the river, she said, there wouldn't be all the need to haul water, such as I had always had to do. I saw smiles among the congregation. Honor the dead. What honors did I have when I needed them, while I was growing up in this cat-box of a town?

I had been sitting on the altar, still imagining myself in the dress I had died in. My body would be buried in the outfit Karen had picked out. There were choices I had never thought about. Karen wanted something a little less *boring* than my bank outfit, the straight skirt, dark-pastel blouse, dark jacket, and plain black pumps. I did have a bright summer dress, flower-patterned silk that I liked to wear at family events, but that seemed frivolous, garish even, against the white lining of the casket. My, my; what to wear? Karen had finally chosen the royal-blue blouse I never wore, one that Arlie and Gary had given me for a birthday. There was a gray skirt, too; that worked because it wouldn't be seen. Pearls. I hope they take them off before I'm put in the ground.

My vantage point made me see the backs of the speakers as they faced the congregation, and I was surprised at how evocative a person's back can be.

Hizzoner, the mayor, Darwin Dixon. He's nice enough, young and from Outside, so that he had only met me as the old fixture on the garden club and at the bank, and a generous contributor to the Letters column of the local paper, noting its hideous mistakes in grammar. "End of an era," he told everyone; I would be missed. His talk had the virtue of brevity, a not inconsiderable one.

Next up, Luther, of course. He numbered my years at the bank—very inspiring. He had been a new man, he told us, coming into a community he hadn't known, but I was there, trusty and competent, with far more gifts than my job description demanded, because of my knowledge of the towns of the Valley. There were relationships between Valley people that no newcomer would have been able to figure out on his own.

I wonder how many of those gathered in the rapidly warming sanctuary were capable of reading between the lines of that encomium. The poor man had spent years in the prison of my superior knowledge, having to pave over his irritation as I vetted candidates for loans or extensions, which, Luther would have had to admit, saved the bank a bundle and boosted his reputation. He was, in a sense, the constant recipient of my bounty, receiving power and prestige without earning them. The recipient of such bounty is seldom grateful, as I very well know, and soon begins to resent his benefactor. I could see him freeze when I came into his office, which wasn't all that often. Sometimes I went in just to ruin his day—"The Tillinghast loan—a good one, I think." "You turned down Steele, I see—good. I know his family. They never saw a lie they didn't like." I often let him know that I had secrets. I never told him what they were.

Here came Larissa, and I lay on the altar gratefully, it being cool. People were beginning to feel the heat and there were still players in the dugout.

Larissa is still well put together, very slim and fashionable. She was here as an Ellie, the sober one of the two remaining Ellies, friends from the time we were eight and our teacher noticed that all our first names started with the letter L. We had little else in common, but like a family, our disparate personalities were forced together into the unlikely configuration of a group identity. LuAnne, the Ellie who died, had been quiet, sometimes, I thought, dull. Had she lived, I think she would have married at twenty, four-room house, white picket fence, small dog, white picket children, one boy, one girl, white picket husband, blue shutters. Lowayne was all laughter, drinking, sixty-five miles per hour in a thirty-five-mile-per-hour life. Was there a color she hadn't seen, a ride she hadn't taken? Let's go! Come on! Larissa had already arrived. She was Doc's daughter; she was pretty and feminine and sought after. Being with us as an Ellie was one of many groups she belonged to. God knows. Without that letter L in her name, she would never have let herself get paired with a tough little party girl like Lowayne or a worn waif like me. Speaking for the clique now, telling the old story, the one no one remembers but was once all over the school, she aimed to lighten the mood.

There were plants in the high school, in the principal's office and on every teacher's sunny window. The plants grew slowly because the school wasn't heated at night and the growing season here is measured in days. I was given the honor, because of my good grades, to go from room to room on Wednesday afternoons to water those plants. I had a small, special watering can to use, and Mrs. McFee, who taught science, told me to water each plant carefully and to report any drooping or yellowing one or any plant patchy with disease or pests.

The honor was important to me and I never allowed one drop of water to fall on a window ledge or the principal's desk. On the fifth of these Wednesday afternoons, I noticed a plant drooping and hanging over the edge of its pot. Its leaves were spotted with yellow. I reported this to Mrs. McFee and she told me to bring the plant to the class right away. Down the steps I went and back up, holding the drooping plant carefully. I opened the door to the classroom and everyone erupted in laughter. Mrs. McFee shot a look of annoyance until she saw that I was genuinely at a loss. "That's an ivy plant, dear," she told me, "and the yellow patches are part of that type of ivy." Another whoop of laughter, which she silenced with a look.

Larissa told the story well enough. People chuckled.

There had been no plants at our cabin. The pictures that showed rural poverty in the children's books we read—*Heidi*, and the Little House books—all described a sweeter poverty than any I knew, one with window boxes and flower pots filled with blossoms. LuAnne's house, where I lived later, had no plants, and because I was never trained to notice such things, I didn't pay attention to houseplants in the places I visited. My present prestige as a gardener represents my rage, tongue stuck out at all those laughing hyenas in the high school. To the congregation, the story made me dear and cute. To me, it was shame on shame. Does everyone want desperately to tape over those early knife wounds?

Larissa smiled and went back to her place.

Global Village, they are calling it. Those people who see something comfy and warm in that term never lived in a village. They drape it in wisteria. They don't know that a village is full of secrets because secrets can't be kept and lie like leaf litter at the end of winter, when the snow draws away and reveals them. How do I know why Larissa came back here after only one year of college, claiming that she was too homesick to stay and didn't like the rush and noise of Denver? Martha Peet, one of her mother's friends, was a woman I visited until she died in 1987. She was in a nursing home in Callan, kids gone every which way, husband gone. Over the years she told me all kinds of things. She told me that Doc, whom I idolized, had had a woman in Bluebank for twenty years, and would have made it longer but for his death. Corrie Bendixen wasn't interested in what she called "The Marital Relation." Larissa and her brother somehow got conceived and born and then it was over for Corrie. Mrs. Bendixen liked being Doc's wife. She liked being what in

Gold Flume went as upper class. They sent Larissa and Kenneth to college, Doc being one of the few in town who had gone.

In less than a year, Larissa was back. She had gone down there as town royalty, wreathed in our admiration. When she got to Denver, she must have found herself hardly the biggest grape in the bunch, her manners provincial, her place of birth the smallest print on the map, her importance non-existent.

She had her beauty, though, among many other beauties. She met a boy and fell, perhaps, in a kind of love. Martha wasn't quite sure about that. Larissa was no student. I think it must have been a relief to her to leave school, marry a man just out of college himself. They eloped, and he must have told her that he had been disinherited, because she never met his family, who, he said, were very wealthy. She never asked, since he had been disinherited, where the money was coming from that supplied their travel and fun. She had told Doc and Corrie about being in love but not about the marriage, knowing they would have disapproved of her not staying in school.

And pregnant. She found, when he disappeared, that the "minister" had been a frat brother and the "home" a house let to him by vacationing relatives. She called Doc, who was town enough not to bring her back here until it was all over and the baby adopted away. Larissa came home with a figure slimmed by sorrow and a story constructed of spiderwebs.

In Doc's generation she would have stayed a spinster in our dying town, but as she had been changed, so had Town. I was married by then, and the uranium-molybdenum boom had hit us. People were coming to ski on Cantin's Hill—one hand-held towrope on a pulley. Larissa stayed. She met Richard Madsen, an engineer at one of the mines, and became a matron of importance. After her children were gone, she went into real estate and gave Karen her first job in the office. Karen would use the experience well.

And her secret? She doesn't know I have it, but it has made me smile many a time when she raised an eyebrow at the big words she says I use.

And my secrets? Well known two generations ago—that my parents, loving, sleepily loving as they were, weren't like other people. I remember them so clearly walking carefully down the ridge of the Hungry Mother, the way to the road, and if they couldn't get a ride in Hannes Johnson's coal cart, walking to town. It's such an early memory, it hangs in sunlight. When they got to town they would go to Henderson's Market and spend the day there, working. Henderson's was the only grocery in town then. I don't know what they were paid;

it couldn't have been much—they weren't worth much as workers. Slow, both of them. Henderson would have to tell them what to do and they would slowly repeat it as they did it, one thing at a time. There were other secrets, too—that I was a slave to the in-laws after Del left, and the big one, of course.

And this funeral service? Genteel as a crystal nut dish. Not a word about suicide, although it was an undertone, there all the time. Everyone went with the Hopeless Illness myth, saving themselves because they never saved me.

TEN
MARK

I'D NEVER HEARD THE IVY story. Lily was a wonderful mother-in-law, but she was reserved, so reserved that you took it for granted. She'd turn the talk outward to us, listening, eager to hear what we were saying, letting us slip past her opinion or experience by giving it a word or two, neither in agreement nor in argument but a third thing, and it wouldn't be until you got home and were revisiting the evening or the day out that you'd realize that she hadn't said anything personal, or that the personal was simply an appreciation of you and your situation and point of view. Lily appreciated; I mean that in both senses.

I didn't say any of this at the funeral service. I spoke generally—how I'd come to Gold Flume and met Karen and been charmed by her. How I had taken an interest in developing the town as more than a ski area. Lily was no small help, there. Many women chat. Lily never did. I'd had some luck with investments and planned to put them into the town's growth. Lily didn't point or direct. It was always: "You might look at…" or "You might try…"

Karen was a good choice for me. We complement each other well. She, too, is careful. I think both of Lily's daughters got that from her. Karen says that growing up in that big house with those two old gargoyles, and then with a widowed mother in this small town, made them almost as studied as the children of preachers.

I didn't say most of that, either, and I certainly didn't talk about Lily's wedding gift to me. She had bought us a set of Revere Ware—those steel and copper-bottomed saucepans. Inside the smallest one were two cards in envelopes, signed to each of us. Karen opened hers and was tearful as she read something sweet and loving, she told me. I opened mine, expecting to read a welcome to the family. There were three simple sentences: Elliot Curson owns the building at the corner of Third and Miner. He is elderly and not in good health. There are no heirs.

These facts were nothing that many other people didn't know, but I hadn't known them, and when I did, I was in a position to make the offer that began my purchase of Prospector's Block on the main street. Lily's friend Larissa also helped here and there, and we've done very well. There won't be any college worries for the kids and I've got a good handle on my retirement, and should have more in the years to come.

I didn't say any of this, either. I spoke of her being a good mother-in-law, loving grandma. I said what was expected. People like to hear what they expect in these situations. Sometimes, when you go deeper, people misinterpret your words, which is why politicians are forced into unambiguous boiled cabbage, pale and over-cooked.

After the service, a little tedious except for Jenny's very moving reminiscence, we went up to the cemetery. Lily's parents weren't buried there—something about an avalanche years ago when she was a girl; I never got that clearly. I also know she had no love for her in-laws and didn't want to lie next to them. She had told me some time ago that when she went, she wanted to be buried in the newer part of the cemetery, a part we—the city council—had acquired and set aside for our increasing population. The old part was bare, except for what weeds and wildflowers were ready in their time. The headstones were in rows, family and family, the way you might sit in church, but there were many random ones as well.

I don't think our kids will live here. The housing is too expensive, the taxes too high. Most of our own teachers, firemen, police, and tradespeople live in Bluebank or

Granite City, down the Valley. Gold Flume's success has sharp teeth.

The trees were budded out and there was a pleasant smell from some of the bushes of squaw currant. The spring beauty was over, but here and there was a pasque flower. Some people had put in plants that could survive the cold nights, sparse water, and a short growing season.

We were all, even in our minds, walking around the fact of Lily's suicide. In all the years I knew her, I never saw Lily when she wasn't completely put together, hair in place, hose and heels. She wasn't vain—she wore no jewelry, and little makeup. Her clothing was simple but her need to be presentable was absolute. She couldn't have let us see her in those hospital things with a urine bag. I believe that the diagnosis would have been disabling—would cause her to take her own life. I didn't put my thoughts quite that way to Karen either. As we stood by the grave I saw the casket lowered and I said, "She died sitting upright, hat on, hose and heels, and in her spring outfit that she wore to church." Around us, the family nodded in recognition, little smiles on their faces in memory. That was as close as we came, or, I thought, would ever come, to her reasons and meanings. It's an old saw that we never know what goes on in other people's minds, and we're always surprised when we find out.

After the burial we went back to Lily's. It seemed natural; the big old house was where we had all spent holiday evenings and Sunday afternoons and summers in her garden, where Gary and I had put in a barbecue pit and built the garage. I don't know what we will do, eventually, but I hope we keep the house for a time, anyway. The place was grandfathered in years ago under a homestead law, so the taxes on it are reasonable, but it will be unrealistic to try to keep it up for long. Museum, I would think, deeded to the city, or even to the county, with us accorded privileges—I'll have to find out what that would require.

ELEVEN
PASTOR FEARING

THESE THINGS, CEREMONIES—WEDDINGS, BAPTISMS, FUNERALS—ARE, to my mind, what the church does best, and this case is the proof. The fibers of the family are straightened and made to go in the same direction through me, acting in sympathy, but disinterestedly. Here's what we do—here's what we say. The rough and raw often comes out later, when the will is read or the house broken up and family possessions assigned and distributed. At the times of greatest change—a marriage, or the final cutting away of one relationship or other—there are things that will never be the same. We are here to ease the way and perhaps give comfort. Lily Beausoleil—people talk about the end of an era; what more could I say? The woman's life was completely dedicated to this town.

Was the church ever what we wanted it to be? Is any institution?

—and for a suicide—there seems to be some question—I used to think that suicide was, in some sense, a private act with reverberations only in the immediate family, a choice among other choices, but years standing over coffins has brought me to the awful accounting that the choice makes. The results for the survivors, except in extreme illness or debilitating old age, are the same: shame, guilt, anger, pain that cannot be assuaged. This collage of feelings does not happen in natural death, death being natural after all.

This one is a puzzle. I can't say I knew Lily Beausoleil well. Ministers seldom get to know people well. Like the police, we stand in a special relationship because we stand for special, stated rules. The police enforce law, the ministry morality. People don't think we can put those rules in the background. A man with a beer can in his hand will freeze momentarily when he sees me and change his language. We and the cops carry parental images and bear the weight of ancient battles in which we took no part.

I know that Lily Beausoleil was a power in Gold Flume, and in the whole Valley, all the three towns. She was pleasant, but one sensed the iron beneath. Her suicide, I think, must have been about age and pain. I get the feeling that had she been in agony, dealing with agony every day, no one, not even her children, would know of it.

—and the house. I want that house. The parsonage is tiny. There are no rooms where groups can meet. The church basement has been given over to the school and child-care center. AA meetings are held with the participants sitting in cut-down chairs in rooms full of pictures of puppies, kittens, and Jesus Christ looking sappier than any of them. The church hall is for wedding and funeral receptions and has all the warmth of the high-school gym. The house is a block from the church. Oh, the plenty: Lamaze in one room, AA in another—of course it will have to be gone into very carefully. There are charity and tax advantages in a donation. Some sort of arrangement might have to be worked out for mutual advantage. We need money.

I'm pleased about what I said. Lily Beausoleil did actually embody something for this community. When there are as many vacationers staying for short periods as we have, the streets are full and the real population must sift through them to find one another. Many times church attendance is increased by out-of-towners—ski clothes in winter, strapless tops and Hawaiian shirts and frayed shorts in summer. People seldom pack for church. Lily was always in place, coming early, perfectly attired, sitting in the third-row pew on the left near the aisle. Her five-dollar bill in the collection plate was always token payment. Lily tithed in private, which was what first brought her to my attention. A tenth of her salary at the bank. It's exemplary, really. Of course, her needs were very modest. I imagine her sons-in-law paid for her utilities and the running of the car, necessary now that the mall is three miles away between here and Callan. She couldn't have been a gourmand or a drinker, or a gambler—town gossip would have told me that. Her needs were few, but I'm sure she could have used the money. Tithing doesn't show, but it sinks a bolt into the structure of things and anchors them. I'll miss that money.

TWELVE
LOWAYNE

I GOT TO TALKING TO Larissa up there at the grave. Over the years, we haven't exchanged a hundred words. After my accident with Charlie that night in March—1953 it was—she dropped me like a hot rock. Charlie and me, we was drunk. Bobby Howland started out driving and went to Aureole, and coming back from Aureole, where we had been partying, up over the pass and down to Granite City, we was singing and he nearly went off the road so many times that when he got to the Valley Highway, we made him get out and gave Charlie the wheel. That was stupid, really, since the road to Gold Flume through the three towns is dead straight. We hit black ice, and Charlie was doing ninety-nine, the cops said. Anyway, the car hit an elk out for a moonlight walk and over we went. I didn't know it then, not until two days later when I was in the hospital and Bobby and his date, Angela, was dead. In those days, lots of kids drank and drove, so Charlie only had to pay a fine, not go to jail.

By then, Lily was living by the river in a shack with Del and a dirt floor. Soon, the Beausoleils found out and put the screws to him, which made him mad so he married her and up they went. She'd been working at the bakery when Del found her and "made her his" to the gape-mouth shock of all of us. There he was, picking her, picking her out of all the dying, fainting, heart-attack victims who followed him with their google-eyes whenever he appeared and lowered his radiance to our streets. He was a war hero, Del Beausoleil was, from Korea, with a medal and everything. And he came back full of that glamour for us. They got married. Up she went to the big house, up there in her wash-yellowed blouse and Larissa's last-year's straight skirt, stockings by Millie, shoes by Claudine, purse by the Catholic Church rummage sale, hat by one of the Van Riper girls. She was gray-faced. Del married her and disappeared. He left her with his folks, the two of them, after twenty minutes or so, to follow up on a job offer. They took her apart. What was the child of two morons doing with their son? No high-school diploma? Nothing to recommend her—borrowed clothes, borrowed food, borrowed life. Did she love him? Yes. "Then do him the favor of not dragging him down. Shed him. Let him marry one of his own kind," they said.

"He says he loves me."

"He loves your pussy, which you must have flashed at him enough to get his attention. He's young."

"He's twenty-five."

"Twenty-five is young for a man. If you think you see yourself as mistress of this house one day, disabuse yourself of that notion. You have nothing to give him. What will it take? We will give you five hundred dollars."

"I have money. I work at the bakery."

They laughed. Mrs. must have been rocking back in her chair with it.

Lily told me all this fresh from the shock, as though the nausea of it had let go. She had to tell me. I was sitting at home, recovering from me and Charlie's ride. I had broke ribs and a broke arm and a lump the size of a golf ball on my head. She couldn't tell anyone else but me.

So the two of them moved up there and disappeared into that big house. His folks stopped her working at the bakery and she got to have a sunken look to her and soon she looked drawn and soon she was pregnant. Lily was small already, small and dark, and one tooth over the others. What her life there done to her made it all worse. She looked hollowed out.

He got work at this and that, but he never stayed long. I went up there now and then. He, Harmon, was never around—he'd be shugged up in his library. Addie—God, that woman had a mouth on her. She would show her power by ordering Lily around while I was there. Her eyes glided over me like I was furniture, but on the few times that Larissa came with me, the old sow would wonder aloud why her dear boy hadn't married Larissa instead of the—I think she once said genetic mistake, which was what Lily was to her. By that time, the female heat of the local girls had died down quite a bit. He was hanging out with high-school kids or one or two of the guys from his jobs. All those were younger than he was—it made us know that there was something off-kilter about him.

The first job, as I remember, was up at the quarry, driving and running earth-moving equipment. Lily was high with it. The pay was good and they would save, she said, and that would get them a place of their own. By that time, she was full-on pregnant and her eyes was shining with hope. The workers had trailers on the edge of town, not far from the quarry, she said, and they might live there until Del would rise, would have to rise, in the company. She told me she would show Del's parents that she was a good wife and that after his success even Addie and Harmon would have to adjust their feelings about her and admit that Del had married well. There was some kind of accident up there and he did some heroic thing she was so proud of—a big write-up in the local paper.

And then, three months, maybe, and Del got fired for not showing up at work. He told Lily that the job was no good. The boss was singling him out for criticism all the time. I remember Larissa and me sitting in the Beausoleil's kitchen and listening to Lily and wanting to shake her. Didn't she see that Del had come back in the first place because he couldn't make it anywhere else? You read *wife* in those days and the list reads loyal, be loyal. If you can, be proud, but if you can't be proud, be loyal, and smiling. Be pleasant. Be thrifty with the money he gives you and don't spend it on yourself. A good wife sends hubby out each morning well fed and well dressed to face the world. If he drinks, her nagging is the reason. If he noses after other women, it's because she doesn't give him what he needs in bed. We all heard it all, and some of us believed it, and Lily swallowed it like a starving person eating—all need.

I was up there more than Larissa, who was even more spooked by Lily's in-laws than I was. Addie actually wanted her beloved son to ditch Lily and marry Larissa, who had come back from Denver, magically, to be a proper mate for her boy, who would then form part of the six-family Gold Flume aristocracy. Now, standing in the crowd at the grave, I said to Larissa: "Do you remember Del's folks and how they wanted you for him?"

"Vaguely," she said. "What were their names? Do you remember them?"

I bit my lip. Here's the drunk, the brain-pickled sot, who remembers, and Mrs. Richard-Only-One-White-Wine-At-Dinner-Please Madsen had forgotten it all. I wonder if she even remembered that she had a kid somewhere that no one knew about, not even her sister and brother. It seems unfair to me that I get stuck with everybody else's bad memories. "Addie and Harmon," I said. "You got to remember that hair, chestnut brown, like wood, a face like Canyon Lands, five foot ten, two hundred and fifty pounds, all of it quivering with indignation. He was tall, too, Harmon, but stooped over like a buzzard, and beaky, and with bags under his eyes, your standard carrion bird. Don't you remember how we asked each other how two such altogether ugly ducks could whip up a son who looked like a movie star?"

She gave me a vague look, Larissa, and said, "I don't...I don't remember."

I remember one job for Del, another, another. Lily had her baby, Karen, and he was gone for weeks at a time, for which the Beausoleils blamed her because she wasn't charming enough to keep him home. Big house, yes, but no washing machine back then. They sent their stuff out

to Ramona French to do, but not the diapers and baby
clothes, and Lily had to do them outside in a boiler in
the yard, or, in the worst of winter, in the basement. Try
to be charming then. There was no disposable anything,
just water toted out to that boiler every two or three days,
to the back of the house and around the side, where the
neighbors couldn't see.

And Del home now and then, so there was another
kid. The plan had been, in his leaving, that he would be
looking for work in other places and would be sending
for her and the kids to set up there in a place of their
own. She told us this more than once, and finally, we
was biting our lips. I was, anyway. I'm not proud of that.
It seemed funny then. I half wanted to remind Larissa,
standing there beside me on the old-snow, new-grass hill,
pasque flowers out and the aspen, too smart to bud in
so treacherous a time, beginning their catkins. I wanted
her to own up, before she moved away to be with better
people than I am—"Do you remember how we laughed
at her behind her back? How she kept repeating his lie
number two hundred and ten with a straight face?"

Jail was what Lily was getting all day from Addie and
Harmon—"Look what we are doing for you!"

What woke her up? What tipped the scales? I can't be
sure, but I do know when it happened. After Arlie was
born, Del's "trips" got longer and longer and there were

two kids in diapers and Lily woke up one morning and got dressed in her yellowing blouse and sagging skirt and went down to the Molinos at the bakery and asked if she could pay them a fee to use their washing machine. There she was, all but shoeless, toting a basket full of dirty clothes. It took all of half a day for the news to climb the hill to the Beausoleil ears.

Uproar. I got this from her later, uproar and yelling in which she sat with an unsmiling set face, until Addie yelled herself out and Harmon was so horrified that he gaped his beak and dropped his dead mouse. When they was done, Lily said, "If you don't want me walking the streets in poverty, you'll see that I get a washing machine to use, or drive me to Molinos' where they have one. If you don't want me saying things to people, you'll give me time in the evenings to take the correspondence course I read about. You'll let me have the money for some decent clothes and for the course, and we'll divide some of the cooking and cleaning chores, or you'll hire me as a cook and maid."

They went dead silent. Lily told me that she heard the clock ticking and the sound of the voices of the kids in the front room, muted by the drapes and the rug. Then all hell broke loose. Again she waited it out, sitting like there wasn't no one else in the room. When they was finished, she said, "Del is gone and now I have nothing to lose. When I go to church or out of the house with the kids in rags, don't you think people will wonder as much about you as about me? What grandparents let their grandchildren go begging? Who lets their daughter-in-law haunt the backs of restaurants and go to the church's clothing drive? I've worn church cast-offs and LuAnne's clothes since I was twelve. I can do it without a touch of shame, but now, when people see me in Mrs. Shoor's last-year's suit, there won't be any protection for you, and I won't have to say a word."

They caved. They sent to Aureole and up the hill come a washing machine. She got an allowance for clothes, and a month later, with just an eye-glance reminder, Lily was sitting at the kitchen table, when the family had gone to bed, studying her correspondence course in bookkeeping. She never spoke a word of criticism about her in-laws, at least not to the world outside our protection. We were still the Ellies.

I said something like that to Larissa. I could see her getting restless, eager to be away. "We did protect her, back years ago when she was living with those two old plague-sores."

Larissa, just for a second, dropped her grand-lady pose and said, "Yes, we did, didn't we—we went up there and visited. They treated you badly, but me even worse."

"Worse?" I was amazed.

Larissa nodded. "They wanted me for their boy, because every time Addie went to see my dad for one of her medical problems, she would urge him to get us together when Del was home. 'That Higgins girl was a mistake,' she told him. 'Your daughter is a fine girl. Wouldn't they make a lovely couple?' I heard—overheard—some of this now and then as she was leaving, but there must have been more pressure from her because one day, when I was ready to go up the hill to the house, Dad stopped me and said, 'Don't go up there alone. She's got an eye out for you. Lily's a good girl who has made a bad mistake and it's good, your looking out for her, you and Lowayne, but except for your visits, and taking Lily out now and then, I'd stay away from that old lady.'"

I didn't know that. Larissa saw my eyebrows go up. She grinned. "And you thought you knew all the secrets in this town," she said. And we laughed.

Living in Gold Flume means that people like Larissa have to learn to live with people like me. On TV they talk about diversity in college and businesses all the time, but everyone knows that a city is much less diverse than a town like this. Charlie told me that. In the city people go to school with Blacks and Jews and Hispanics, the very religious and the atheists, but the minute class is over, you are with your own—same opinions, same races, same wealth. Larissa knows my life. I know hers.

She went to school with their postman; their kids and grandkids with a rancher's kid and a banker's kid and the son of Sheriff Valken, who is now sheriff. There are Republicans, Democrats, far right, far left—maybe only one or two of each, but they can't get away from 'diversity' the way city people can.

Burial is over. I need a drink and maybe a nap out on the porch after. I'll miss the reception, at which I would be as welcome as a case of the clap. I paid my respects. I move on past the groups chatting. It's been a while since the last death in town, and people are catching up in the very pleasant sunshine where a little breeze is wreathing around them, cooling people off after the crowd-heat of the church. I move off past the little groups and on to the road. No one stops me or calls out for a word, or comes after me for a final comment that would link me to Lily, whom I have known for all these years. It's not that they consciously ignore me; it's that after years of being ignored, I have stopped existing.

THIRTEEN
LUTHER HAYES

I WAS IN MY OFFICE early on Thursday. We had been to the funeral on Wednesday. It was such a nice day that we had gone out on the patio. I had my headphones on, listening to the last half of the game. Betty was reading. Betty is not a peaceful person. I hadn't been married to her for a year before I knew that if present circumstances didn't upset or annoy her, she would find some that did. Yesterday even she seemed peaceful.

We live in a gated community here, in a new development at the far end of the Valley up toward Prospector Pass. The houses are set on five acres of land with splendid views of the mountains. The house is twelve thousand square feet with an exercise room, his and hers work rooms, an entertainment center, hot tub, and four bathrooms. The master bath has a sunken tub and shower that can spray from twenty-four nozzles built into the walls of the cubicle. We've spent a fortune furnishing it in what Betty calls California Mediterranean: big, chunky furniture, purposely crude. The slipcovers were made out of near burlap and dyed in "earth tones," whatever that is. There's a huge kitchen, capable of turning out meals for fifty people, although we seldom entertain, and then no more than two or three couples. The house cost two million five, and furnishing it three hundred thousand or so. Sometimes I think that all this is a bit pretentious, but a bank president has to live up to his means. People expect it. Ours is a second marriage for both of us. Betty's two kids are now in college. We didn't have any of our own. My three are in Philadelphia with their mother. The two lived with us more or less normally until they were grown. I can't honestly say we were close. They never rebelled or went heavily into drugs—they slid away, smoothly as one muscle slides over another in the actions of living.

I guess funerals make you think about such things. The tellers and secretaries were still talking about the thing when I came in. Whenever a major bank officer leaves by retirement or for another job, the audit is moved up so that the new official starts out with a clean slate. Lily B—Mrs. B—was hardly a major officer, but she filled the job of one, working here from the time when the bank was doing loans for ten-thousand-dollar houses and businesses, land sales of two or three hundred dollars. Now, we have complex loans of ten or fifteen million on homes, land, and businesses. We have two bookkeepers and our system works well. Of course much of our smooth operation depends on her intricate knowledge of the Valley.

I'll be making changes now. I'll put my own stamp on the bank. I'm looking forward to that.

FOURTEEN
FEDERAL AGENT STEVE PECKAR

WE GOT THE CALL FROM an auditor up in Gold Flume, Colorado. Good deal—great fishing up there, swimming, hiking. After working dozens of cases in cities, I was ready for a little fun. The kids were out of school, so I thought I might combine a vacation with the job. A week, I thought. It couldn't be much—small town, little money available, little old lady, Harv told me, hand in the cookie jar. We all went up there in a holiday mood.

How wrong I was. Sometimes the problem is best seen working forward. This old broad had been here for forty-two years at play in an expanding playpen.

It's a long valley with four towns between Victory Pass and Prospector Pass, which someone told me used to be called Jackass Pass but had a name change when the gated developments went in up there. They tell me that if I'd gone up to some of those towns in the thirties, I would have thought the whole valley was dangling on the edge of death. But in the '50s Gold Flume had begun to retreat from the cliff edge. They started mining strontium then, and uranium and molybdenum, going over the old mines and the tailings from the gold and silver veins that had been mined out. The '60s brought skiing and the area went into serious promotion as a tourist destination. Bluebank, once a railroad company town, got rid of the crumbling company houses and the cribs outside of town and built a museum. A school for sophisticated artisan crafts was built and became internationally famous. Callan still mined, its extractions very specific and secret, and there are fortunes made there. Gold Flume hosts three arts festivals a year and brokers architectural contacts between private and corporate clients, drawing architectural designers from all over the world. In 1980 two Japanese billionaires and a few Middle Eastern sheikhs built huge houses on the cliffs—east and west—that looked out over the valley where the Ute River didn't look like anything that could eat a pathway through these corridors of stone. The sheikhs had houses with fifteen or twenty rooms in which they housed their harems, servants, and entourages.

I got all this from a chatty lady at River Walk, the place by the river where there is a plaque that she said will have the old girl's name. Apparently, Lily Beausoleil was one of the driving lights of the place; very pleasant it was, too, with a stretch for joggers and bikes and with set-aside places where benches shaded by lilac and aspen and cottonwood have been set up. The dame I was talking to was older, I'd say in her sixties, so she didn't have a cell phone attached. I'd gone down there at a suggestion from one of the bank secretaries.

All this was after having changed plans, called the CBI office, and told Harv that what we had here was no little old lady who had missed out on her bingo prize and dipped into the petty cash. After I finished with him, I left the motel and went to the chamber of commerce, where I told them that my stay would be not for days but for weeks. The lady there put me in touch with a family that rented me a room with two meals a day, something normal in what promised to be a hunt through some heavy timber. Harv said he was sending Soderburgh, who'll want to stay at the hotel. He's young and he's gay. I want the stability and ordinariness of a family. As soon as I found out how much there would be to do, I sent Marie and the kids home in no particularly good humor. We'd spent a nice four days, but I had to tell her that I had no idea of when I'd be home. I call every day and talk to both kids, too, and Marie is used to me spending weeks, even months away.

Most embezzlers use one or two of the common ploys—dormant accounts or skimming. This gal used more, many more. The bank's computer records go back only to 1980. The rest of the material is in boxes of yellowing paper. After realizing what I had, I decided to work forward instead of back, as we often do. She started out in 1955, six years before I was born. I was joined on Tuesday by Soderburgh, who was, as I had figured, well set up in the hotel off Main Street. He had gone online and found a gay group, which he called an outpost.

Gold Flume is not what it was when Lily Beausoleil began her career. The old mining and ranching days are kept on in an effort to supply the fantasies of tourists. Trips to the mines are in full swing and many of the ranches now run on tourist participation—people seeking experiences they feel put them in touch with something more active and basic in a life that was gone before any of them were born.

So Soderburgh and I began in the musty ledgers in a dozen boxes in 1955 when Lily, a young mother, got work in a small, quiet bank with small quiet loans and a remarkably low percentage of defaults. I don't think this speaks to a higher morality at the time, but to more caution in lending. She's straight as string. '56, same, '57 same. We do this in two days, spending most of them sifting papers, and by 1960, we've gone on microfiche and things go faster, but I have to admit, at the loss of some of the flavor of the time and the way things were. Sure, there are the records, the transactions, the money involved: six hundred twenty acres at two hundred an acre, very big business back then, and only a few of those going through. Houses were being sold for ten thousand, some older ones for five. College loans? Very few of those—one in '50, young woman went on after high school. Thousand-dollar loans. From Ms. Lily, not a glimmer. She gained in status all through the '60s, signing more, being given more to do, but the bank itself was growing. The ski area opened in '62 as more than two rope tows up a mountain. People who had come once began coming back for the beauty and atmosphere of the place.

It was Soderburgh who saw the first one, one she must have been seeing up close for some time before she acted on it. It was a dormant account that she'd signed off on in the name of a relation, a little ridiculous, since the man was in his nineties and had designated no one as his heir. The account was for six hundred dollars. Nobody looked into the withdrawal, which was made on an especially busy day. Everything balanced. The slip had been made out in the spidery, unsteady hand of an aged person. The man was a Jotham Lally. He had actually been dead for years and had no relative remembering him. There was another. Low-hanging fruit. The next year there were others, light stuff, but there. The money began to move between accounts, accruing interest that was moved again before it was noticed. She took none of it, only watching it grow, attaching it to other accounts as it grew. That was in the 1963 and '64 years, her launching. By 1965, she had accessed two larger accounts whose owners she must have known would never make a peep, died, maybe, or moved. The amounts weren't over one thousand dollars. Altogether, with the money garnered from interest, other dormant accounts weren't large, nowhere as large as is seen these days. Then, they would have been considered serious. We called our offices—how much could this woman have taken? The current scams run to the billions, taking leagues of forensic accountants and FBI agents to unravel. Did they want to waste us on this?

We were both comfortable here, I think. I was fishing after work or early in the morning, Soderburgh partied. On weekends, I flew home, making up the hours with longer days. People knew we were bank examiners, and the second day we were there, Town knew it. Someone floated the rumor—I think it was Hayes, in a smart move—that we were researching a possible merger. No one likes the idea of fraud. People get nervous about their money.

Word came back that both of us were to stay on the case.

June arrived, and in the middle of the month, great clouds of pollen blew through town. The pollen yellowed all the surfaces the wind knows, and caused antiphonal sneezing throughout the bank. At the Williams' house where I was staying, there were cookouts and barbecues with neighbors and friends and gentle and occasionally not so gentle attempts to question me about the bank merger. Sometimes Soderburgh joined us. I liked the family, the kids, too, in spite of the occasional adolescent sulk. Our own kids are years away from teenage, and the message I hear is that I should relish these years I have with them as they are.

Now and then, I'm moved to ask some questions about Lily Beausoleil. Who were her friends? I have been wondering what happened to the money. How much has gone into the town? The Williamses moved in five years ago, and wouldn't have known her as anything but The Woman At The Bank In Town. Their own bank is the new one at the mall.

I did ask about the town, though, in a general, friendly way. Yes, they told me, there were levels, the migrators and stayers, the new people and the old, the money people and the less than super-rich. Everyone not grandfathered in by the 'Homestead Statute' has to be wealthy, because land

and tax values are so high. The underclass can't stay here at all, except as live-in servants of one kind or another. The rest stay in Granite City, in trailers.

We had Lily down pat in 1967, then, and '68. By that time she had about twenty-five thousand, and then the money disappeared, coming back three months later, almost doubled. "Call the other banks in the Valley," Soderburgh said, "she's lending it out—"

She had begun playing with varying interest rates, too, and there was suddenly a lot more money. From where was it coming? I began to study the sources and I found them in the public records office in Aureole, the county seat.

There were powers of attorney, thirty or so, granted to her, starting in the late '60s and ending two years ago, with a senile old man in a nursing home in Bluebank. Soderburgh was incredulous. Were there that many people around here with no relatives, no lawyers, no other fiduciaries?

Somewhere in notes, in someone's reminiscences, I'd heard about Lily's visits. Hayes and others had told me that Lily had upheld the bank's image as community minded and "caring" by visiting all the old-timers, people living in prospectors' shacks and cabins of hermit-like solitude, or the dry ruins of the communes of the late Back to Nature years that had brought the inept of the cities to farm or ranch on land whose only harvest was mineral salt and rock. These communes had come and gone back a generation ago, sometimes in a matter of months, leaving a few ragged holdouts to pull bare existences allowed by the penurious rain.

One day late in June, I'd gone up to the cemetery to track some names. I was impressed by how many single individuals were there, how few family plots. These days with everyone being cremated, the town stories, the who was related to whom, will be gone, files to be kept without the chords, the harmonies of these places. Even the cities will be cut from the score, a symphony played one instrument at a time. No wonder modern scams blow into billions. No one can see a full picture and the links are all submerged in the ignorance of strangers. Lily knew. I wondered as I walked among the graves if everyone knew in those days, who was worthy of trust and who was not, who lied and who didn't. Computers are supposed to bring us all that knowledge now. They don't. We are ignorant of the twining of lives and relationships. We are, in the words of my grandpa: "Dumb as a barrel of hair."

FIFTEEN
LILY

My amusement at Town's misunderstanding of me is tempered, I find. I've always thought that I didn't wish to be understood, and that no one would understand, in any case. I had awakened from my trap all those years ago, married to a man who wasn't there and in-laws who were, poor, a form of servant. I found two ways to escape: my job at the bank, and Harmon's library. It took me ten years to read every book in it. The books a person reads are a key to his personality and his dream of himself. Harmon was, in his own mind, an intellectual. His library labeled him a pretentious snob. I never saw predilection, preference, tendency in him, a favoring of any style or writer, any sense of delight that gives a person the feast of enjoying all the books of a favored author. His library, and it was a very good one, was purchased from lists: the 200 Essential Classics of Literature, the Great Works of Western Minds, World History (seven volumes). I read them all. There were good and not so good translations of the Greek and Roman writers, human history as one walked into the room; on the right and moving around the room one hit the Renaissance fairly early on in the first bookcase, separating in the second into English, French, German, and Italian, and at last, on the far left, coming to the Americans with Hawthorne, Melville, Emerson, and on the last bookcase, modern. Many of the books opened to mine as the first eyes perusing them for more than a glance.

My education there was one more secret from the town. I kept that secret, too, because as my plan was slowly unfolding, I needed people to see me as ordinary, and except for living in the Beausoleil house and being in the garden club, not exceptional at all, not in any way. After finishing Harmon's library, I had to order my later selections through the small library at Granite City, a library which was the living room in a private home, presided over by a woman who, with her readership, kept only paperback romances. She never noticed what she passed on to me as part of the inter-library loan from all over the country. I wanted no one to suspect that I was an educated woman.

Habit often takes me back to the bank. I've been shocked but not surprised at what people have in their safety-deposit boxes, and I'm privy to all the work that goes on, slipshod sometimes.

Here they are, Steven Peckar, FBI, a big, young man, only now beginning to thicken and go spare on top. Fisherman, soccer enthusiast, dedicated father and husband, and very good with figures; his companion, Miles Soderburgh, wry, a gay man playing the field, but an intellectual heavyweight, and they are calling me gifted, even brilliant.

I have been spending most of my time with Peckar and Soderburgh. In the beginning I looked in on them now and then, simply to see whether they were finding any of the strands of what I had been doing for all those years. Their enthusiasm began to charm me.

It was early in July, hot and dry, with the valley floor turning from luxurious green to dangerous brown—wildfire time, day-blaze heat watering up from the roads and withering what had announced itself in the optimism of May. I was in the bank with them two or three days after they had begun to see the discrepancies that made Peckar, tracing a roll of entries, cry out to Soderburgh, "Look at this—look at what she's doing!" He said it with such enthusiasm it was almost as if he was rooting for me. I smiled, hanging over them to remember those early attempts of mine. So I wasn't a silly old broad—I had heard the Old Broad appellation and had been offended when it was said. Now, the same words were used with surprised respect. "See this—here…here. No wonder she never missed a day at work. She couldn't. She was all but channeling the adding machines."

Then, later in the week, they came upon the first power of attorney designation. I was lying above them, supine, like a figure on a monument, when I heard Soderburgh say, "What control—she never loots an account." Peckar nodded, saying, "There are land transactions that she cuts into before they're registered. She changes the amounts for the interest variations and waits no longer than a week between the money in and the money out, putting everything back after a venture. False name, here…I wonder how many more she used."

"Thirty-eight," I told them both in a whisper into the air-conditioner that was saving them all from heat stroke.

They were working back in the '60s, late, before the big money began to come. That didn't happen until we got people of really great wealth here, a full arena for my talents.

I remember it so well—I had forged Keller's name to a withdrawal slip, having seen the signature was a very easy one, but I thought to go and visit him to make sure he wasn't going to come in to the bank and cause trouble. When I went up there—a prospector's shack on Jackass

Mountain—and saw that he was barely alive and was living on cans of potatoes and beans the grocery sent up once a month, I asked him if he didn't want me to handle the payment of all that from the bank. He was only too glad. I came up with a power of attorney document, which he signed. He paid me with an irregular disc of pounded gold. I visited him every month until he died. I used another name when I sold his land.

And there they sit asking one another if I doped or gambled or had a man somewhere with a taste for pleasure. I laughed at that. How could those well-favored men even see into a life like mine? A man—where would I keep him, in the attic?

Once or twice, I've been tempted to float over to Karen's house, or to Arlie's, but at the last minute I turned away. I know they miss me. The grandkids do, too. We dream, egotists that we are, of parents and grandparents looking down on us, nodding their approval at our successes, saddened by our losses. I myself have, or, rather, once had, those thoughts during those first years when I told Addie and Harmon that with the girls in school, I would be using my hard-won and well-earned certificate in bookkeeping to get a job at the bank. They hadn't noticed that I had improved myself through recourse to Harmon's library and that I had Doctor Bendixen's recommendation, that I was well spoken and appropriately dressed. I thought how proud Mami and Papi would have been to see me claiming my place for myself and for their grandchildren. They had been poor and illiterate, hounded and fearful, but they had known how to love and they had loved me, in their way.

I haven't visited my daughters or their families at all, out of a delicacy I didn't know I had. Perhaps I thought I had made that up, too, my pose of unassuming gentility. Heaven knows I devoured those etiquette books I got from libraries—what to say, how to eat, how to accept, how to refuse. I built it all, layer on layer, the way I used the gift I had, the gift I used to get justice from the people in this town.

But there are people I love here, and I want them to have the privacy that had been denied to me, to go freely about their days, even though they would never know that I was floating or flowing curled up beside them, listening. Those ghosts we summon out of our pasts to be proud or sympathetic aren't there to watch us on the toilet or picking our noses.

Now and then, I did visit homes, and those visits were increasingly boring. I had always envied Larissa, first as Doctor Bendixen's daughter, a rosy, golden life, I thought, warmed by his approval, rich enough to wear her own clothes, sleeping and waking in rooms that echoed approval and choice. Even after her disastrous year in Denver, and her knowledge that there is a child somewhere, and possibly grandchildren about whom she might wonder in her hours of sleeplessness—I...the word is envy.

Larissa has made a very advantageous marriage. She has a maid and a more-or-less handyman to paint and fix and tend her fashionable xeriscape. She doesn't work, but sits on various boards and has book clubs and a personal trainer at the country club gym. I spent time with her in all those places. I realized that she would have been in the garden club, too, where many of her old friends were, except that I was the president of it. Some shared pasts are not as comfortable as could be wished.

The garden club is not what it was. The founding members, those grade-school friends who stayed in Gold Flume, are ailing, dying, changing downward. Larissa thought us too dowdy. She doesn't garden; she has a gardener. It is enough, she thinks, that she had voted as a chamber of commerce member to okay the beautification project we did for the downtown back in 1990, looking toward the millennium, and for the continued beautification of the town.

I didn't visit Larissa to hear what she was saying about me, or to dine on any memories she would share with friends—after our young girlhoods, there would be few enough. I found myself nostalgic for a life I hadn't had—ease, leisure, the well-cared-for garden, tended by someone else, long summer Sunday afternoons, games. I've hovered over a dozen afternoon and evening games, cribbage, chess, mahjong, bridge. I never had the time for those games, the party games. When I wasn't at the bank, I was at home, keeping the house in order, dusting, sweeping, seeing to my clothes. I also did the essential visits, and of course I had had to look after the girls when they were growing up. I never formed the habits of leisure. This didn't stop the pictures that formed in my mind—those pictures of women having lunch or tea together, and weekend barbecues and backyard events, which are really for couples, so that even if I had been invited, I couldn't have come. The bank had a summer picnic out on the river near Bluebank to which I went once or twice, but only when Karen and Arlie were there to play with the children of the other employees.

Now that I'm dead, and with no work waiting at home and no defenses to guard, I find myself gravitating toward strangers' summer fun: kayaking down the Ute, fishing, outdoor games and pleasures. After looking in on Larissa once or twice, I found I was happier with tourists than with Town people. Slowly, in their own summer dresses, the aspen and cottonwood, the wild maple shrubs and water willow enfold me, and wind-rocking I can cease from hating this town and its people.

So those whom I visit now are people whose secrets I do not know. I stay away from my grandchildren, also, as an act of love, and so that I will not stumble over their selfishness or stupidity. Would I intrude if I had the power to warn? I don't think even then. My suicide made two statements. It was a way out, a quick exit before the building collapsed around me, and a thumb in the eye of the people of Gold Flume.

Now and then, I have experimented. I could, if I wished, be breathed up a nose or into a mouth and then up into a brain, resident in this one and that one as he or she went through a day. Brain, yes—thoughts, no. Now that I do not have a point of view, standing up in a body, senses, gender, age, relationships all hooked up and interacting with a world, I see how elegant it all is, and I have been floating into church on Sunday to pay my respects to the Creator of it all. In my late sixties, a lot of that marvelous body hurt, especially in the early morning, but there was also the unappreciated joy of action, movement, the heat of coffee, cool water on a hot day, all the body long. Could I be mellowing? I hope not.

I spent the week, much of every week, at the bank learning a great deal and seeing even more clearly how character and personality play into even so objective and impersonal a business as finance. And, of course, a daily update on the works of Lily Higgins Beausoleil.

I relished each power of attorney. I got this one in my name, that one in others. I remember some; most I've forgotten. Linthicum, the bootleg prospector working other men's claims in secret, a wrinkled lemon of a man who kept snuffling as though he were smelling out someone else's ore sample. I remember how he tried to question me about other people I knew. Were any of them prospecting, too? Where? Were they getting anything good?

What surprised me there was how few of them I remembered, how few of all those I visited could be summoned up. There were standouts—first forgery, first power of attorney, first mattress full of money I found, the corpse inextricable from its bedclothes, first visit in Callan, first in Bluebank. I was surprised and a little chagrined—I'm proud, maybe vain of my memory— every transaction for forty years, but the people—I remember ten or so—no more. They spill and merge into one another, dissolving. I never realized that until this moment.

SIXTEEN
LUTHER HAYES

OF COURSE I KNEW THERE was something wrong, even before the auditor called the OCC man and the FBI. We've had the usual audits—they took a day, files requested, called up, everything checked out. This time there were requests, and more, and more—by the end of that day Jacqueline was hyperventilating and Lucia was crying. That had been Wednesday. By Friday we knew that what was happening wasn't a glitch, some transposition of figures by mistake, the now-and-then misapplication of accounts—checking to savings. I called the board. It's a mandated thing. State law. We all stewed over Saturday and Sunday and on Monday the stones of the rockslide had begun to land. I had no idea the slide would tear away half the mountain.

I tried everything to keep the news in-house. I told everyone that we might be getting ready to merge with the big bank in Aureole, which has just gone with Columbia National, which is huge and with worldwide ties. They have all kind of requirements and red tape, I said, which necessitated all these inspections. I never said FBI and the FBI man didn't either.

But after the first few days, rumors began and our board had to be told something more like the truth. They didn't want to blab, either. Nobody wanted to blab, but ignorance talks as well as knowledge and the two men sifting for days in Mrs. B's old office and their requests for the hundreds of files and entries got the secretaries and clerks talking. The tellers told, as we used to say, and they had mothers and fathers and friends and before long, rumors blew into established fact—the bank was being sold to a foreign conglomerate, Betty told me, a combine that would dictate from Europe and/or Asia at a huge disadvantage to the dollar.

People are out more in the summer, socializing. Rumor goes further in the warm weather. I was hearing half-words and being asked bits of questions at cookouts, or interrupting hurried sentences when I came up to small groups. I got significant looks. Betty's friends, she told me, were asking her questions. Which was it to be, Asia or Europe? Was it international Jewish interests?

Should they ready themselves for some kind of financial panic? Betty also told me that I wasn't helping things by going around with a—she said—hunted look. Of course it was the damn Beausoleil woman. The Feds didn't tell me, but they weren't getting records from the '60s and '70s, five managers before I came on, for their amusement. Lily Beausoleil was the only employee who was around in those days, and around until a Sunday last month. We had thought, at first, that it had been a heart attack or a sudden stroke, and then Betty told me that it had been a suicide because of a diagnosis of some awful condition, something fatal and incurable. I began, as the summer went on, to suspect that her suicide, if it was a suicide, had nothing to do with any physical condition and everything to do with the mandatory retirement from the First Bank of Gold Flume, formerly known as the Miners and Ranchers Bank of Gold Flume, the name it had been when Lily Higgins Beausoleil first came on.

And, of course, while Peckar and Soderburgh were there, none of my plans could go forward. I couldn't even get rid of her office and use the space for our computers and backup files. All my plans were on hold while those two went through the records so old they still bore the steel-engraved logo of the pick, gold pan, and branding iron of the old bank.

And they began to look at me, with looks that seemed to ask where I had been and what I had been doing while this woman plundered accounts right and left. A manager manages. I've told them what they already know, that managers go with the figures presented to them if those figures are consistent day to day, month to month. I've been feeling defensive, which I shouldn't, the embezzlement starting before I was born. I also began to resent a kind of admiration they seem to have for her underneath all their careful, bland superiority. I was passing her office where they are now working, piles of papers, trays full of files, and two rolling carts full, and Peckar was saying, "Look at this—look at her go, just long enough to get the rate differential."

Soderburgh: "It's the control—coasting for three months, pulling out the difference. Here's another dormant account…"

"It's one she's used before."

I stood there, stopped by the excitement in their voices.

Soderburgh said, "And then there are these powers of attorney, five or six of them, and they seem okay when you look—she skims; she's careful, and there's always something left."

"Greed kills. She's never been greedy, even when it was dangling within reach."

They were enjoying it; I swear they were.

"Fifty thousand made of shavings over fifteen years, quiet as a bat pissing on velvet."

"By 1970 it was sixty, and here it comes, I'll bet the ranch on it."

"What do you bet it's going to have to do with land speculation?"

Admiration. They were giddy with it.

Their designation—federal officers examining our operation—kept them from dealing with us as equals, supposedly to keep chumminess from influencing them and to cut down on potential bribery, but it also encourages secrecy and a defensive atmosphere. I kept feeling that I had to prove myself.

I suppose I've brought some of these feelings home with me. Betty has been angry and on edge, snapping at me. She tells me I've been picking on her, criticizing, coming in late without calling. I tell her it's work, and it is, but I can't tell her what it's like to have those men here, scrutinizing everything, with the careful, cagey look when they have a question for me. I tell myself it's not about me. Those dusty files and brittle tapes have a generation on me, made when I was investigating my playpen. My career hasn't been meteoric. I'm no genius, but my progress has been steady and the Gold Flume Bank is…has been very well rated and quite influential for an institution of its size. Anything higher would have to be in a big city. No, I won't get the blame, but I will be caught wearing the clothes I had on when the shit hit the fan.

And it's summer. We should be traveling, maybe visiting the kids, or touring. I had planned to take Betty to Sweden this summer—my mother's family came from there. I'd even begun to research which village they had come from, planning to go there and then to Stockholm and maybe even Paris or Rome. Of course, now, I can't leave—it's nothing they've said, but the anxiety is beginning to permeate the staff. I watch their movements and their stances and gestures seem stagey to me. There's less chat among them, none of the banter I used to think was inappropriate for the staff of a financial institution. Now I miss it, and the easy way they had with the patrons, which has been replaced by caution. I heard a number—sixty thousand. How much more can she have taken? Sixty thousand is money, sure, but a sixty-thousand-dollar bank robbery wouldn't be seen as top priority. When will they leave? When will they finish up and leave?

SEVENTEEN
ARLIE

I NEVER THOUGHT OF US as having privileged childhoods, but in a way, I guess we did. There was very little money; Karen and I both worked after school and summers, but we had the big house and everyone knew us. There did get to be an upper class in town while we were growing up, but it was small enough so that we got included in it by default. Most were the kids of Mom's friends. The new people were all much richer, but many of them came and went, regulars, but summer people, so we still had an influence that wouldn't shrink until the '80s when the really big money came and the two- and three-million-dollar houses went up on Jackass Road, now Prospector Heights. Even then, people moved in, spent three or four years, and left, building the influence of the town but not influencing it themselves and not being influenced by it. Older people came, too, for luxurious, quiet, big houses with just the two of them. I've been making some very nice money selling those houses. I got to be a realtor without actually wanting it as a calling, and found myself working high-end homes and land, and liking it.

My position is what got Pastor Fearing over to see me. He wants Mom's house for his church. He wants us to donate it. He was investigating the idea, he said, just to see what would be of advantage to all of us. A sale, he told us, and any other buyers would tear it down. The land it stands on is simply too valuable to support a single dwelling. He got animated then, like you do when you have an idea all of a sudden, a breakthrough, a revelation. He had heard about the homestead law that protected old houses and big land homesteads. There's an exemption in the law for one-owner land, contiguous acreage and home owned by one family for over fifty years. This real estate has an exemption for property willed to heirs, and here's where his eyes lit up, or to a non-profit institution. I was grinning inwardly. He had heard…he had heard, my dead cat. He was able to quote section by section the laws pertaining to the house and the dimensions of every damn room in it, of the land it stood on and the minerals beneath it. He must have been studying up on all of it before Mom's body had been taken out of that car. The poor sap's eagerness blinded him to the obvious. I'm a realtor. Did he think he was bringing his homestead statute to me like a triumph—the way my cat presents me with dead chipmunks? I'll give him this: the facts of Mom's suicide stayed out of the gossip mill longer than I expected and I know that if he had wanted it to be otherwise, he could have dropped enough hints that would have charged it up like an atomic pile.

Meanwhile, Karen and I had been going up every Wednesday to check on things at the house, and we had hired Alicia's boy to go up and mow the lawn and weed the garden. Melody Reimer had told us prissily that the garden club didn't do weeding and never had. Lily had done it in her own garden, and the club members had a girl for the flower baskets downtown, but there were no plans to do more than care for the flowers. I told Pastor Fearing what *he* already knew, that Lily's garden was a major supplier of flowers for the church. He would have to get someone to weed it and keep it while we decided what to do. So it was garden club versus Altar Guild, ten rounds, bare knuckles, with Pastor and Dick Crane on the town council as referees. I had unwittingly been the cause of uproar between the two groups. The Sunday after Mom's death, I had approached both. Each thought I had given it the nod. I had, in two months, managed to gum up what had been perking happily along for forty years. I had thought of them working together. Good luck.

Fifteen years ago, Marissa Benson, the film star, and her current husband had bought ten acres and built a five-million-dollar, fifteen-thousand-square-foot house on Silver Creek. I sold them that land and soon two of her friends, also film stars, bought adjacent parcels and built similar mansions. Money had been dribbling into town from skiers and summer people since the late '60s, but the presence of celebrities made it boom. Before we knew it, mountain and town realtors had more work than we could handle. We hired two more people and another secretary. The celebrities drew others, the merely rich, and in a few years we found ourselves with problems and problem clients we couldn't have imagined ten years before.

They wanted an airport. They wanted an airport that could accommodate private jets, that had state-of-the-art features. They wanted rapid computer access, cable TV, and power grids that could handle any and all of their needs. They wanted all the electrical lines buried so that the scene presented was 1890, not 1990.

They wanted to keep the two-lane highway, but they wanted it perfectly maintained. They wanted luxury, discreetly hidden, shopping, food and wine, but not in Gold Flume itself. Outside of their own acreage, they wanted the land kept pristine, but the ski area people, who had been there first, became a competing interest as condos walked up the four mountains. The boast of most of the luxury condos was that the buyer could ski to his door. The lodges got bigger. There was neon downtown before we forbade it, after the two years in court that took. Both the celebs and the skiers wanted a variety of upscale stuff, restaurants and clubs, but the skiers also wanted Wendy's, McDonald's, and Burger King.

Aureole is the county seat, so most of the howling arguments took place there, over Victory Pass. A dozen lawyers would find work through the decade, as the titans went at each other. As I think back to that time, it seems to me that Mom was the only one who kept her equanimity. Everyone in town was on one of the four sides of the war: pro-skier, pro-celebrity, pro-year-round tourism, pro-closing the town except as a destination spot, which could be done only by not widening the highway and by discouraging motels and cars within the town limits.

We all took sides, even within the family, Karen being Town and Gary and I being Realtor, and all our friends being either ski-area- or star-crazy, not to mention all of our young people taking sides as their jobs at the ski area or with the other celebs dictated. Even the garden club got in on it.

Mom alone didn't seem to care. We read the *Ute River Voice* avidly for every blow-by-blow and report of every meeting. The *Voice* itself had gone from a four-sheet discussion of the school lunch menus in the four towns, who got married and who died, to a full twenty-eight pages with two full pages of letters to the editor, some of which were scary in their mindless rage.

That was when we were refreshed on some Sunday afternoons at Mom's, birthdays and holidays. It wasn't her cooking, God knows. Mom must have been raised poor. She never talked about her folks except to say that they lived on the Hungry Mother and died in an avalanche when she was away visiting in town. I pictured her at a sleepover. I knew that her mother and father worked at the grocery that used to be here and that I remember only vaguely. He must have brought home the produce they couldn't sell—the sprouted onions and rooting potatoes, dented cans, gray meat. If she had had to write a list of pleasures, I don't think food would be on it, and I know she never cared about cooking. She made our meals when we were growing up, but dutifully, following the recipes that were simple and cheap. We always watched the pennies—canned fruit for dessert, canned vegetables or, later, frozen, mac and cheese, hamburgers on a bun. If we brought home a recipe from a friend she would make it, once.

Our friends' houses often had welcoming aromas—onions browning, cakes rising in the oven, comforting bread baking. Town women went through food fashions following the TV of the time—our versions of Julia Child or Yan—but Mom was at work and didn't want the fuss of elaborate meals.

What was her source of pleasure? It wasn't food or play and she wasn't very social. Church, garden club, her fellow workers at the bank seemed to satisfy her need for other people. She saw them, but almost never socially. What delighted her? We did, and beyond us, order, the fitness of things, appropriateness, nothing in excess. A summer purse and a winter purse. Matching shoes, modest suits, one for summer, one for winter, these were her wardrobe, changed with scarves or pastel blouses. She line-dried her wash and took it down the minute it was ready. I've seen her go out three or four times to test them for dryness. She was punctual—to the minute. When she looked around and saw order everywhere, her face would relax and the small muscles around her mouth would spread and ease, and would let down, and there would be a smile of pleasure, a warmth, and a little nod. Yes. Yes.

Gary remembers the wonderful meal we had when he first came to the house. I never told him that Mom didn't make it—we did, Karen and I. Over the years, we made or brought all the holiday meals we shared. Now we both have kids with all-too-well-educated and expensive tastes. Gary and Mark were part of Mom's sense of fitness as well. Both the men are good-looking and wear clothes well—the grandkids, too. We are very lucky that way. Mom died before the messy adolescence of her grandchildren, the green hair, the sullen, pierced lip. Gary and I have been married for fifteen years and we have our three kids; we are stable people and I believe our marriage is stable, although a look at the news on TV any night would give anyone the willies about the longevity of anything.

I'm wondering now if we shouldn't have separated from Mom a little more to make our own ways in the world. Mom and her life and death should mean sorrow, grief, but not the overwhelming sense of displacement and loss that it does for us all. She really has been the hub of our family, the wheel of which we are the spokes. The wheel won't fall off the cart now that she's gone, but I've been feeling the wobble—a sickening kind of lurch.

EIGHTEEN
STEVE PECKAR

EVEN WHEN SHE DID THE standard stuff, our girl did it with flair but never with flamboyance. In the 1970s and '80s when the building boom started in town, she went slowly, fitting her moves to each situation in so slow and measured a way that none of the ordinary pitfalls that could lead to detection touched her. Soderburgh admires her restraint—I admire her memory. I would compare her accomplishment to…a great orchestra conductor, perhaps, who knows each individual part in the score of a full orchestra for dozens of works, or a racing aficionado who has the bloodlines of hundreds of horses and their performances on tens of tracks for hundreds of races all in his head.

Our admiration is a dirty little secret we share, Soderburgh and I. God knows, most criminals are stupid, their work transparent, their only protection the laziness of superiors and gullibility of their co-workers or the apathy of their regulating agencies. They're unmasked by their own greed and fecklessness. Pinson bought a million-dollar house in an upscale community and had a hunting lodge in the Cascades, all on a postman's pay, and said it was an inheritance, having once or twice boasted of his humble roots. Demos got drunk and told all to a mistress whose greed was greater than his and who blackmailed him. Compton took off for sunnier climes and went as far as Deming, New Mexico, where he stuck out like a crocodile at a dog show. A diet of that kind of perp dulls inspectors and makes us wonder if stupidity isn't more pervasive in the population than evil and isn't worse.

Where is the money? Why did she steal? It's not in her lifestyle, on her table, in her closet. There's no evidence that she left this Valley except for one visit to Denver with her garden club in 1990 to visit the Botanic Garden's xeriscape display and take workshops there. We find no contact with gambling—she has no home computer and didn't do any private chat online at the bank. The computers she used are clean as whistles—Maartens came up from Denver to look into that. Where is the money, two million by now?

In the 1980s she began working her several scams with land deals throughout the Valley, in Callan as Callan began building ski condos, in Bluebank and Granite City as they began to flourish with the ski area in Aureole and Gold Flume. Interest in specialized mining came back to Granite City then and she was behind several dummy companies there. Soderburgh says that had she been living in New York, she would have gotten billions. My view is that it was the specific knowledge she had of this Valley and its four towns, plus Aureole on the other side of the pass, her absolute understanding of every person and event in this Valley, that gave her the gifts she used. Her time and place fitted her exactly.

She's dead; we can't ask her. I do have a theory; I can't see it any other way. I tell Soderburgh and he says he's been moving toward that idea since we learned that she had never done any foreign travel. The money is here. We'll get agents to toss the house. Of course that will require paperwork, a court order, just cause, etc. We'll still be working but we'll give our agencies a heads up. She may even have the money in the attic somewhere—two or three million packaged in hundred-dollar bills, five thousand worth at a time, wouldn't take up too much room. It would be heavy, though, lots of suitcase-size boxes light enough to carry. Where would she store them? The money is not in paper. It couldn't be in paper. It would be gems. It would be gold. We think it's two million, but since the fraud has been gaining as the years go by, maybe more. We know that there's no evidence of her using any of it. Therefore, yes, the house. There will also be other evidence, books, lists, all those dummy accounts in other banks, lots of lists. Many neurotics secrete money in parts of their houses, waiting for a government to collapse. Some, and I've had a few of these myself, are so fearful that they put the money in dozens of accounts in banks all over the country, often losing track of when and where and what names they used. I don't see our girl doing that. She was a careful person, precise as the dot under an exclamation mark. She must have lots of codes and numbers in her head, more than I ever knew from my other perpetrators, but there's a limit to what a single brain, even the brain of a genius, can compass. Idiot savants run on very narrow tracks, deep, but narrow. There must be lists. I don't see her burning them before she killed herself either, but if she did—it would have been that Sunday and there'd be evidence. I think there are packets, boxes of evidence, names and numbers. She had, over the years, so many dummy accounts, dormant accounts, some partly looted, some breathed in and out on a regular basis. There are numbers. Somewhere there are the numbers.

NINETEEN
LILY

I'VE BEEN SILENT FOR SO long that I've almost forgotten what sound I might have made. I have forgotten, or maybe never fully known, how the girls loved that house. I only know how I hated it. After Harmon died and then Addie, and we had torn down those dusty drapes and gotten rid of their smells, and the smells of their hopes dying, the girls were full of joy. I sat at the kitchen table and figured and my figuring told me that I couldn't sell the monster. There would be no buyers at a price that would give us another place to live, a place near enough to the bank to let me walk there and back. There were no condos then, townhouses, apartment complexes, only wretched rooms over the stores on Main Street, most without electricity or water. The heat in this house was supplied with coal, uneven in winter, and the maids' rooms at the top of the house where the three of us had lived were not insulated and could go from freeze to bake in a day. The house was too big for us, a total of twelve rooms and four bathrooms, plus halls and three sets of stairs. The kitchen was huge and there were two pantries and a vast collection of dishes and serving equipment. I knew how hard all this was to clean and keep; I had been the maid here for years.

But there was no other place to go. We all moved down to Addie's and Harmon's rooms and closed off the upper floor. I went into the second bedroom and gave the two girls the master bedroom because my memories of my in-laws were too depressing for me to sleep comfortably there.

We had no money to replace the ugly, heavy furniture, but slowly, over the years, we did get new mattresses. I found all kinds of things hidden in Addie's old one—money, sixty dollars in all; two corroded hip flasks with the brandy dried out of them; women's magazines, four of those; buttons; and a pair of white calfskin gloves, beautifully made. We replaced the pillows and recovered the couches and chairs and, with the help of Lowayne and her boyfriend Charlie, and their friends, moved the unwanted furniture upstairs to the attic.

The house echoed like a canyon, the hardwood floors sounding at each step. Larissa gave us the old carpets they were replacing in Doc's house—someone else's castoffs one more time. The whole house was someone else's castoff. My bank clothing had been the only thing that had not belonged to someone else first. With my first real money after Addie and Harmon died, I purchased new clothes for the girls—two outfits each, which they wore to school. In the hated house they wore what I could sew on Addie's old machine.

But Karen and Arlie brought schoolmates and friends to the house and they made cookies in the inconvenient kitchen and put up preserves. In the year Harmon took to die, I had stiff-armed Addie into getting an electric stove and oven to replace the wood-burning one we had been using, the hot, hard, inconvenient monster I hated. We were easing. As practical as I am, or feel myself to be, I knew even then that my options were few and that as many bad memories and feelings as I had for the Beausoleil house, it was my only wealth. I hadn't realized that for the girls, the house was a standout in the neighborhood, not the eyesore it was for me; its inconveniences beloved eccentricities, its hand-me-down, faded pretentiousness rich tradition and special charm. So we stayed in the Beausoleil mausoleum, which I so hated and the girls so loved.

And now, to my great delight, men have come in and pulled out all the drawers, those the girls had emptied when they left, one after the other, those that still held what they had not yet sorted and taken to the church rummage, bound for the Charity Grateful in Africa. There were still the house linens there, kept until they should decide about the house. My closets were opened, my blankets and sheets and towels and face cloths, the girls' rooms where the years of grandchildren's overnight leavings still stood. They fingered the gifts I had been given over the years, Limoges ladies and woven porcelain Easter baskets and grade-school gifts of clay and stiffened construction paper cards, their edges parting. They opened packs of birthday and Christmas cards and pawed through them while I watched and laughed. My sewing room, the pantries, all.

And then there was the attic. They were busy all day on that one. There were three men in what we would have called Hoover aprons—gloved like surgeons, looking for secret panels, and auscultating Addie's treasured breakfront, pounding the backs of drawers, and looking for taped lists on the undersides of the furniture. I lay in the air above them and laughed until the memory of muscles in my diaphragm ached with it. The men were focused, intent as dope-sniffing dogs, eager, open-lipped.

And, of course, my trunk with its years of deeds from the Beausoleils and receipted bills and tax records and the house taxes and everything saved in special envelopes, all marked and in sequence. It's a blessing, really, being able to let someone see my dedication to my planned revenge, discipline, order, precision, rationality. I am honoring my father and my mother, Commandment Six, my parents, who went each morning at the same time, to work, to do, with full, utter concentration, what they had been told, and who, in their shack on the Hungry Mother, went through all the routines they had been taught at the pitiless institution of their raising. These things they did with unerring fidelity, unappreciated and unmourned, except by me.

All day the men searched and nothing to show for it. Where were the lists of names, account numbers, the packet of account books? They didn't know that their own literacy had doomed them to overlook my capacity for memorization. Rote memory, everyone calls that, waving it off. That dismissal has unmoored their ability from all its benefits. Oh, dear, oh, dear—could these modern technical wizards with all their electronic gizmos conceive that all of it was stored in mnemonic codes and braids of relationships I built up over generations? Remember, Peckar and Soderburgh, sitting in your cubicles at the bank while your war-dogs break our furniture, that I started with only one and then two, and built by accretion, patient as a spider and as silent, moving along a web I had made. What I have hidden you will never find. I could, if I wished, recount it all, all the numbers, move by move, name by name, to the year, month, and day, into your rock-music-half-deafened ear if only you could hear my whisper. It's all still here, all of it, ropes of relationships. You have gratified me by calling me a genius—Lily Higgins.

When did it start, my embezzlement? You don't know that, or why. *When* was September 24, 1962, and where wasn't at the bank at all, but at Henderson's Market, in what would be its last handful of years. The store had expanded to double its size since my parents' day, and it had begun to stock some few fresh fruits and vegetables and a freezer that held more than ice cream. I had been standing in the farthest east aisle, putting paper towels and toilet paper into a shopping basket. In the next aisle over, the one with the canned goods and cereal, Carol Dunphy, Barbara Sackett, and Evelyn Barnett, three friends of Larissa's, who went for upper class in the Valley, were chatting. I had waved to them and exchanged a word or two as I left the store when they were coming in, and then had realized that I wouldn't be shopping until that Friday and had gone back in for paper napkins and a box of Kleenex. I heard the three of them in their talk, Larissa's name coming up. Apparently she and Richard were going to Las Vegas for their anniversary. I was interested. I hadn't spoken to

Larissa in some time. Then one of them said, "Didn't Lily Beausoleil look good? She's coming up in the world." I smiled. It wasn't my attire. I was wearing a white blouse and dark skirt—maybe it was my manner that had made her say that.

"My, oh my," another voice, Barbara's I think, said, "she's only a clerk at the bank."

I wanted to say, "Actually, a bookkeeper."

"The town should be proud," one of them said. "Those feeble-minded parents and then we all took her up when they died, and looked out for her. My mother practically dressed her." (Lie!) "And the Reeds, all *they* did for her, taking her in like that, and then the Beausoleils, so she didn't have to work in the bakery. They treated her like a real daughter-in-law." (Lie!) "I hope she's grateful."

"Of course she's grateful; she'd have to be, clothed and fed and given a life, even after Del died."

I stood in the store until they left. I was trembling. For long minutes, I couldn't see or hear, except murmurs that receded as the three of them moved away. I felt sick. Grateful. It came to me with some force that I had been asked to be grateful all my life. People who had given me stained sweaters and outgrown shoes required it. Addie and Harmon, who used me as an unpaid servant, demanded it.

Was I ever grateful at all? I suppose in the beginning I was—that Sunday when Doctor Bendixen came up the walk at Lowayne's where we were sledding on cardboard down her sloped yard. I remember one of us asking if anyone was sick. He went into the house and came out soon after. "Lily, will you walk with me a little?" We went down the street, a new blanket of white on the older gray fallen the week before and icy in the freeze-thaw of the days between. He told me about the avalanche and the end of what had been my life. "We'd like you to stay with us for a while," he said. Doc's wisdom was that he seemed to offer things, not demand them. Of course I was grateful, then. Who wouldn't be? I had no clothes but what I had on. Larissa was two sizes bigger than I was and Mrs. Bendixen didn't want me wearing them. Maybe she realized how silly I would look in them. I thought then that she didn't want the clothes cheapened by my wearing them.

LuAnne had died three weeks before that day, and the Reeds brought her things over and asked if they could take me. I was grateful to have clothes. I realize now that giving me those clothes must have been painful for them. There was no doubt in my mind, then or now, that they wanted me to be LuAnne, to replace the sweet, passive, feminine little girl they had lost. I see now that even making that mistake they must have had to inure themselves against the pain of seeing, coming around the corner or coming out of school, a little girl in a dark-green coat with a light-green scarf and the fuzzy white earmuffs.

Gratitude must be like the bread I wrapped and handed over to the customers at the bakery. When it's fresh, it's delicious and has an aroma evocative and precious. As it loses that freshness, staying day after day, the sweetness becomes unpleasant, even cloying. Gratitude kept over.

I had been cloyed to death with it, nauseated by it, and when the nausea cleared, something fresh and welcome as the relief of cold water on hands blistered from a session hoeing or weeding or raking on a hot day. I wouldn't call it revenge; I would call it a need for justice.

I had seen holes in the way things were done at the bank. No one looked at dormant accounts back then. No one questioned that an alert bookkeeper could play among the depositors' savings and checking accounts, pulling them back and forth to take advantage of their varied rates of interest and siphon the difference into the dormant account of someone she knew to have been dead for some time.

I became an accountant to the dead. I knew who had heirs and who didn't. I knew whose heirs had left the Valley and forgotten the pittance remaining in a savings account. There were seven of these when I started. They were bits of the detritus left by the withdrawal of the individual and small-claim prospectors, hundreds of whom had scoured these mountains back in and before the depression time, placer mining for the alluvial gold on Goat Creek or the dozen little torrents that feed through these mountains to the Ute. Some still dug there and left new tailings beside the old ones, getting enough, only enough gold to keep them afloat. Some, more knowledgeable, looked for other things, geode, agate, crystals of quartz, mica, for a modest living in hard times. All of them were gone by 1965, when the big molybdenum and uranium companies came in. Ten were still in the Valley, none mining anymore. Four were in Bluebank and Callan, doing subsistence things. Six were still up on their holdings, getting the old-age pension from the county.

I took to visiting them, and I would visit for the rest of my life, in rest homes, or remote mountain cabins, perfecting my knowledge of the people whose lives and situations had faded from memory and were invisible to the new people coming in on paved roads.

As I grew, I stretched. I found that I could secure multiple loans where the borrower only knew of one, which he was happily paying off while I managed the others. I also slipped from one to another at more favorable rates. Since I knew there would be no default because I knew all the debtors, I also knew which ones would never be alerted by the difference of hundredths of a decimal point.

And as I grew, Town grew. From considering twenty thousand dollars a large account, we saw our average accounts become two hundred fifty to three hundred thousand and some higher, including CDs and other bank offerings.

The early staffs weren't as equipped for the new transactions as they should have been, but I was. I began my career in hate and anger, but the game overtook me. In the '70s and '80s I discovered the roots of what Peckar and Soderburgh would be calling my genius. The way to do what I did was to make maps in my head with lines, each tied to a mnemonic series that would encapsulate entire parts of the picture. Where each amount of money was was one string, at what time another. Where it was to go was still another, how it was to go, another line. Each morning as I walked to work, I planned for what line in the series I would concentrate on. Those were the days before computers kept all the access information, and even then I would keep the double-entry books in my mind, and very different sets of information between bank records and my lines. How could I have known in those years, when I was sitting dead-eyed with exhaustion at Addie's kitchen table grinding out workbook answers in my bookkeeping and later my accounting classes, how much fun I would have, how much wit there was in this, how much play.

I was underpaid at the bank. I was hired as a bookkeeper and not until the 1990s was I given what I should have been earning as an accountant. Harbison did that. He was a good man. Because I was underpaid, I was underestimated, a very strong position from which to work. Being underpaid and underappreciated also kept my anger cold and clear.

I think, though, that I lost something in my loss of trust after the Reeds had taken me and the Beausoleils indentured me. When the new people came in, I didn't trust or like them any more than I did the people already there, whom I knew.

Karen and Arlie surprised me by deciding, both of them, to stay here in town. I had guarded myself against the pain of their leaving for so long and had done it so well that when they returned from college, each a scholarship student, and told me that they wanted to build lives here, if they could, I knew a joy I had never expected to savor.

They had done very well, both of them, with their scholarships and summer jobs and part-time work, supplemented by what little I could do. By that time, I was looking over my shoulder at the trail I was leaving.

I could have paid their way five times over, to any school in the country, but I opened the door and used only one—Linton Barr, a man who had died in 1930, a dormant account into which I had breathed in and out in a very modest way for years. It gave the girls a clothing allowance.

I suppose I'd stopped looking at the town by then. I was seeing it as it had sealed itself into my reality—the row houses near the river where the railroad workers lived, the tarpaper shacks of driftwood and brush just upstream from where it bent to come past the town, the squatters' camp in a gulch by the bottom of the Hungry Mother. I knew we were growing; year by year, I had seen it overlay what had been there, blurring its ugliness and the poverty. I saw replacement of old, small houses by big new ones in town, the creation of three and then four developments around the core we formed, but what the eye sees, the mind sometimes denies. In another decade it would become difficult for anyone to trace the old roads, swallowed by the new highway, reconfigured with bridges and smaller roads into the developments. A decade after that it began to be difficult for the children of the town to afford places there, taxes being so high and the cost of living double that in less desirable locations.

And my own status amazed me. I had been an unconsidered person in town, a responsibility, a drain on compassion and resource. And then, without my noticing, I was Mrs. B, the one who knew, the one who, with a word or two, could change the course of a loan, yes or no, on its way or dying on its paper. No one else knew, except the president, or, later, the manager, who had caused the outcomes. My prestige grew because the early executives were locals as I was, and although no one knew what I knew, they did know something about the personal lives of their neighbors. More often, paper has been made to lie, and new computers can be made to distance people from reality, as the banks offer ever more plans and functions. I've seen new holes form before my eyes. Where it was safe I slipped into them.

I never imagined that death would begin to be boring. I was happy enough to find myself free of body, tiredness, appetite, the need to excrete. As I aged, that last urge had become more urgent and persistent. All gone now, none missed. I rest on the air without the need even to spread my arms for the uplift, the way a bird must.

I've begun to think of leaving the Valley, at least for a while. Why not go to Denver to visit museums and galleries? Why not go to Blackhawk or Cripple Creek to watch other gamblers and see what they have made of the numbers they use at the casinos? I hadn't thought that I might incorporate, get a body, maybe more than one. I've worked too hard at the personality I had, and my interest in the world seems to be dwindling, person by person, place by place. I can't go, not yet, not until my game has played out and Town, which has gotten my thumb in its eye all these years, knows it.

TWENTY
STEVE PECKAR

SODERBURGH'S RESTLESS. HE'S DYING TO get out of here. It's been almost six weeks, long for him, for me, too. Most embezzlements are pennywhistle affairs, sound the note—better yet, there's a Chaplin flick that has a blind girl getting hold of a string on Chaplin's coat, which we soon realize is part of the knitting of his underwear. She pulls and pulls until she has a ball of it. Most embezzlement is like that; one pull and you're off to another case. Soderburgh's nightlife has also soured for some reason that he won't or can't discuss. I suspect that the group he'd found were vacationers. Most of the population here is time-stamped with an expiration date, short shelf-life, intensely here and as intensely gone, replaced soon and then, suddenly, not replaced.

I'm everything but physically at home. There are cell phones, Facebook, Twitter—I have them all and am in more contact with Marge and the kids than I was when I was physically on the scene, but I've been realizing how unsatisfying my situation is. Their compacted Twitter words say everything and tell nothing. I'm talking on my cell phone, but it's chatter, because I'm walking or shopping and she's shopping or driving or on the john. Context and meaning are flattened—they call it multi-tasking, but speech, communication, shouldn't be a task. Even if the minutiae of the days, the basic blocks of living, are all in place, real contact thins out to angel-hair spaghetti.

One of our great moments might be at the table when the kids have gone away to their friends. Another is half-drowsily in bed before we sleep. With the kids, it's here and there, often when we are working chores—raking leaves, changing the oil in the car, cleaning downspouts. After, sitting with Cokes, or a beer for me, when I can be shown, for a few moments, a very few moments, into the landscapes, the harder, steeper slopes of their days. Thinking these things, I don't know what made me look over at Soderburgh and say, "This money is with the kids. The kids have the money. We go after the kids."

* * * * *

Few people are absolutely clean. There's the debt that was incurred and forgotten, money intentionally or unintentionally put into or taken out of two accounts to pay a single debt. In honest people, these things are nickel and dime, a fee not entered, a misplaced check. We weren't looking for fifty-dollar lapses, or, in people with multiple sources of income and multiple accounts, discrepancies. We would be searching for hidden accounts, accounts like those the esteemed Lily caused, as she raised the dead or caused death among the partly living in six-month intervals. Cayman and Swiss bank accounts can be traced even though they are numbered rather than named. Soderburgh perked up. This week we put in for court orders to search the homes, computers, bank accounts, and safety deposit boxes belonging to the two couples, four named individuals, and for any accounts in the names of grandchildren of Lily Higgins Beausoleil.

Of course, Hayes, the bank manager, is finished—not his fault, but he didn't catch the embezzlement or the embezzler; I'm not all that upset. The guy is no great intellect and not the nicest. I heard him in his office cursing her for a full ten minutes when we showed him what she had been doing during *his* tenure at the bank. His curiosity was all about his possible prosecution and the damage to his reputation

And where is the money? What could she have done with all that money?

TWENTY-ONE
KAREN

THEY WERE AT THE HOUSE early in the morning when I was getting ready to leave for work—two men and a woman, grim-faced, uniformed and gloved as though our household things might be contaminated. They had a warrant but they didn't explain or answer any of our questions. I was terrified. What was this? Did they think we were spies? I kept saying, "But you have the wrong people." Cold faces, cold eyes—"Ma'am, you'll just have to stay away and let us do our jobs."

"What jobs? Those are my papers, my books. That's my husband's—"

"You might as well tell us what you have; we'll find it anyway."

"Find what?" I called Mark. "Could we be arrested? Was something planted?" I began to go crazy. "They told me nothing." Mark told me to stay calm. He was coming.

The search went on. They went, methodically, room by room, commandeering all our computers, demanding tax records and any financial materials we had, keys to safety-deposit boxes, all our keys.

We have boxes of keys, keys to trunks, keys to old houses, keys to cars we no longer own. They stripped our bookcases and tapped the walls for hollow places, scarring them, screening them—for what? Were there charges against us? Didn't we have a right to know what the charges were? No, they said, because there were no charges, not yet. I couldn't leave and I couldn't "impede." I could only stand there while they rummaged in the freezer and pawed the piled sheets in the linen closet and left the house carrying piles of records, pictures, statements, diaries, and all the computers, even the ones the kids had.

Mark came, thank God. He stopped the man who seemed to be in charge. Maybe it was because Mark was a man, maybe because of his lawyer's manner, but the man showed his warrant. They were searching the house for money or the evidence of money supposedly stolen from the First Bank of Gold Flume.

It was all wrong. They were all wrong. I began to laugh. What had we to do with stolen money? Mom worked at the bank. She would have known if there had been anything illegal or underhanded going on there. She had managed the books there—for years. She would have known.

I'd heard all the rumors about something going on at the bank. Arlie called and said men had gone into her office and withered her with questions: how much, how many, where is it, the money. What gifts had she received? They would find it all, they said, and when they did, we would go to prison unless we were forthcoming with them now. Forthcoming about what? She had tried to ask them what they meant, what money? And it was "Where is the money," and, "How much is it, or was it in some other form, jewelry, diamonds, maybe, or gold?" It was all crazy, and they were crazy, she told me.

I was off the phone only a moment or so when they came back and began to question me. I didn't know what to do, or whom to call, someone to come and help us. Mark was in another room being questioned. I was terrified and then angry and then terrified again. One of them said, "Your mother's a criminal, lady, and a liar. She might have lied to you, too, family money, a bequest. It's a lie. It's stolen money and we will find it and you will all go to prison." They were yelling.

Then I was yelling. "There is no money. Mom had no money. We have no money. We earned what we have and you are crazy." Then I got up and left them and ran in to where they had Mark and I pulled him up and we started to run to the door to get away, but they blocked us. By then, we were all screaming.

I began to think crazy thoughts—might I run upstairs into our now disordered bedroom, push the bed against the door, and make it out a window onto the roof of the garage? I would have to jump down the back, the part closest to the ground. Could I lock myself in the bathroom, and when they broke down the door spray them with something? Instead of doing any of these things, I went into a corner and sat down, put my knees up to cover me and put my hands over my ears, still screaming until I heard no other noise than my own.

…and stopped. They were all standing, staring at me, all pointing, all sweating, because the day was hot and I hadn't turned on the air conditioning. We don't use it while we're at work.

Men can't do what I did, huddle and scream, unless they are at the very limit of their horror, but the two thugs realized that they weren't going to get anything more out of me than they had, unless they changed tack. "Who are you?" I asked. "Do you have names?"

"We gave them when we came in."

"When two other men were taking our possessions away, I wasn't listening," I said.

"Spiller," one said. "This is Gralton."

"Do you have the right house?" I asked.

"Your mother is Lily Higgins Beausoleil."

"My mother is dead."

"We know that."

I was still sitting in the corner, knees up. "What do you want to know?" I asked.

Gralton got that "I'm being patient" look. "Where is the money?" he said.

I took a big breath. Mark, who had been standing between the two, said, "You can take us apart and you won't find it because it isn't here. It isn't anywhere. I don't know what you think Lily—my mother-in-law—did, but we know she never gave us money. She had no money. We do have multiple bank accounts, Karen has hers, I have mine, and we have a joint account, to which we both contribute. We have stocks. We have municipals; we have some land near Bluebank that we let out to ranchers. We are saving toward our daughter's upcoming college expenses. Our daughter has a babysitting job and money in an account she just opened. All of these are at the Gold Flume bank, Lily's bank. We get monthly statements. The statements reflect what we have added or spent each month. You'll find they agree."

Spiller had caught his breath. "People try to lie to us all the time. It never works. The jails are full of people who have tried it."

"Congratulations," I said, before I could stop myself.

Mark had recovered a little. He helped me up. "The point is that what you think we have or know, or did, is mistaken. You've searched our house. You'll search my office. You can dig up all the land we have and find nothing, because nothing's there. We have no secret accounts abroad, the Caymans, Switzerland, anywhere else. You will go through our accounts. You will look at what we spend and what we save and you'll see that there are no yachts, no diamonds. We have no costly habits: racing, gambling, drinking, or dope. It just isn't there. It wasn't there at Lily's house or in her life, either. *Your accusations make no sense.*"

I knew that other agents would be at Arlie's house. Arlie has a mouth on her and Gary is much more fragile than Mark. He might not be above becoming hysterical and confessing to anything simply to get them to stop screaming in his face.

"We're going now," Spiller said, "but we'll be back. In the meantime you need to get used to the idea that lying to us is bad business."

They left. We stared at each other. I saw something close down in Mark, something freeze at his core. He hadn't been able to protect us. An essential vow he had made to himself sometime in his teens had been betrayed in the moments those bullies had been at us, destroying me. For me, this hadn't been my ultimate hour, that capitulation. "Mark—"

"Not now," he said, and went upstairs. In five minutes he was down. "We have to go to the office."

Other agency people were there also, commandeering the records of every transaction and both our computers. "When will these computers be returned?"

"When we've checked them out."

They were suspicious and uncaring; one, a woman, hard as steel.

We went up to Arlie and Gary's and found that Spiller and Gralton were there, and our presence more suspicious than our very believable wish to warn or commiserate with my sister and her husband. We learned what the FBI thought we had done. We were actors, they said, in a conspiracy to hide millions that Lily Higgins Beausoleil had stolen over a lifetime of embezzlement. The whole thing was incredible, ludicrous, mad. It made me look at everything I saw as unreal, wavering, heat-waved like a mirage.

Where could we go for reasonable answers? My mother was dead. The board at the bank would be in defensive mode. Mark kept saying, "It doesn't make sense. It simply doesn't make sense. She would have to have kept hundreds of accounts and transactions in play, changing, balancing—it's not real."

The men kept at us: "Where are the records?"

Everything we did gave the air of a seeming guilt. We called our lawyer. Mark had told me years ago that lawyers don't defend for themselves. Our lawyer, John Krell, whom we had known for years, seemed as frightened as we were. We talked to Sheriff Valken and called the FBI office in Denver to find out what we could about the inquiry. We called two board members who themselves had been questioned and who hung up on us. There seemed to be nothing we could do, no way we could prove that we had no part in whatever those people thought was reality.

I spent the next day at home, trying to put the house back in order. Some things had been broken. Luckily, Jenny had been staying overnight on her babysitting job and Evan had been out camping with friends. When they came home, they both knew that something had happened, but our explanations eased none of their anxieties. The words we had to use to frame the thing were too complex and incredible for them to understand. We saw the confusion and fear on their faces. Evan was weeping. I wondered how many houses they had seen ransacked on TV, how many police questionings? The reality was so different, so fearful, so traumatic as to fuel their nightmares for years to come and make the once interesting TV show a cruel joke. Mark and I told them what we had decided on. The authorities were looking for some proof of another person's crime and thought we had played some part in it. This criminal might have programmed a virus—they both knew all there was to know about computer viruses—and that was why Jenny's had been taken. We were certain there had been a mistake, which would soon be corrected, apologized for, and forgotten.

With the impounding of all our computers, our business was shut down and our home life severely restricted. We decided to go on vacation. Gralton had told us that we hadn't been charged with anything. If that was true, we were free to go, to travel. Why not take in Mt. Rushmore and the Black Hills? I'd always wanted to go there. We asked Arlie and Gary if they wanted to come with us and bring the kids. We tried to show enthusiasm about a summer trip together. They said yes.

The day before our trip, Arlie called. Gary had been complaining of chest pains and she had driven him to Aureole. He was in the hospital there, being tested, and while they said his heart was basically normal, his blood pressure was extraordinarily labile, too high and then suddenly too low. When the admitting tech asked him if he had been under stress lately, he burst into tears.

"We wanted to go with you—we both thought it would be good for all of us," she said, "but the doctors said his condition is too risky. As soon as they get him under some kind of stabilization, we'll be able to go. Why don't you take the time anyway and get something new to stare at? Do you know anything about what's happening?" Arlie's voice sounded lost, almost childlike. "It's some kind of awful mistake. Was Mom really a spy, selling information about our nuclear capabilities to Nigeria?"

The joke was off. She sounded wan, but I answered it. "There's a secret code. You tap on the hot water pipe in the old house at midnight—one for yes, two for no."

"Mom wears a wig. She carries the information in a vacuum cleaner filter bag, one with a special lead lining."

We weren't laughing when we said these things. There was a tiredness we couldn't overcome with jokes. Spiller and Gralton had been too fierce, but it was good to speak out loud about the ridiculousness of the whole thing. Couldn't they see? Where was the evidence, any evidence, a dollar unaccounted for in our house, our car, the kids, our vacations? Did we lose at a casino? There was nothing.

I'd gone around and around all of this day and night, picking at the sore until it bled again and again. I wondered about permanent harm to all the kids, Arlie's and mine. We'd raised them with such care, terrified by ourselves and by experts telling us that bullying anger or harsh judgment could scar their lives. Their worlds had been carefully planted and mowed and barbered by us and our neighbors, teachers, doctors, ministers. We went over their ground with metal detectors, probing for land mines. They had no true language or expression for so great a powerlessness as we now faced.

Mark and I, with a protesting Jenny and a stunned Evan, drove up north and west to Portland where he has cousins, and we went to the Chinese garden, a miracle of peace and harmony in the middle of the city, and to the Japanese garden, proof of what genius can do with five acres of land—when there's water for it. We wanted to feel ourselves on vacation, holiday, but we weren't paying attention to any of it. We were listening to other voices, seeing only what we had left. Now and then, Mark would explode in temper or brood and blow on his resentments. Instead of letting the anguish go, I would answer or demand. Jenny and Evan picked up on our anxiety and added to the exhausting stress in their own way, Jenny sulking, Evan whining.

Our accounts had been frozen—we had no money and Mark's cousins had to pay for everything. The more we protested our innocence, the harder they looked at us with dubious eyes. I knew they were wondering if there could be an embezzlement without us knowing anything? Wasn't the town small and didn't everyone in small towns know all about their neighbors? What had begun as a refuge, gracefully offered, ended as doubts on their side and bitterness on ours.

I kept telling everyone. Mom couldn't have done what they said she did. She had lived in that old house as her sole inheritance. We would have known had there been a penny extra. I would have seen different food on the table. Jenny would have been sent to private school—a range of gifts on birthdays would let us know, Christmas would have been far different than it was. Where was the money? It wasn't on the table, or in the closets. Good God! She didn't get a color TV until we got her one.

TWENTY-TWO
LILY

WHAT ARE THEY DOING? CAN they do it, go into the houses of people who played no part in what I did? I was alone, all those years, you dimwits, you idiots! My good wishes, my good disciplines are being used against me. I didn't hear about those raids on Karen and Arlie and even on Jennie until I dropped in on my Feds and learned what they had done. I had been up on Hungry Mother trying to inhabit a hawk. I was on vacation from Gold Flume and all its people. The bird became conscious of something not itself among its feathers and kept trying to dislodge me. Birds are more intelligent than we think they are and nowhere near as lighted-hearted, playing in the air. After learning that, I couldn't stay. I wind-drifted back home and to my FBI men and then I flowed over to Arlie's and watched her and Gary sitting at their kitchen table like two ghosts, staring at each other. I heard him say he was sorry for what he had said in the heat of anger at being betrayed.

"It's a mistake," Arlie was almost screaming, "all a mistake. How could Mom have had all that money and we not known, not shared any of it? We had budgets for everything. Both of us had summer jobs. Both of us had scholarships to the schools we went to, state schools with no extras. Find a dollar she or we didn't earn. Find one we couldn't identify or document to the penny."

I gathered that this wasn't the first recital of the modesty of her raising. Gary was sitting, listening to it with a look on his face that made me turn away and curl into the air current from their ceiling fan.

It was borne in on me suddenly that all the people—all I could think of, who might have understood what I had done and why I had done it, were dead now, or had moved away, or had never understood. The one who might smile a little smile and nod her head knowingly, was sitting drinking slowly and steadily, her brain plugged with plaque: Lowayne. She would know. Go over there and get Lowayne to tell you what had happened. When you know, you will understand, and when you do, you might even find the answer.

In any case, I'm sure Karen and Mark, and Arlie and Gary, will be able to account for the wealth they have.

The only advantage I ever gave was in what I suggested they do with what they had. I did as much for every bank president since Bob Mackler back in the '80s.

I began to wonder if, sliding up into someone's brain, I could influence his thoughts. What if I got into Peckar's skull and told him where the money had gone and that no one knew, certainly not my daughters or their husbands, people who loved me and whom I love. Knowing where the money is will tell anyone who has known me why I did the things I did. Even Larissa, who didn't deserve a father like Doctor Bendixen, and who can't take hot showers because she can't stand having her mirror clouded even for a second, might be torn away from the contemplation of her own serene self to think about what she and the town did to me. I want to try to see if I can break into a brain and send a thought, a picture, a message. My daughters don't deserve the blame they are getting.

I began with a child. I suppose I thought the way would be easier. I chose a girl I didn't know—one of the daughters of the fancy pastry chef who bought out the old bakery the Molinos used to have. She was a cute girl, bright enough, I thought. I went in through her mouth, spreading up the lattices of her sinuses and finally reaching the inner dome with its leathery dura that protected the treasure of our species. I circled myself up and into the mass of folds and pulsing tissues there. Nothing. Now and then there were parts of the organ that would flutter with activity as the child, who had been pulling a little cart in which a doll sat, talked to herself or to the doll, or turned around to see where they had been.

There was only that, the thick, putty-like substance through which a slight current of electricity thrilled here and there, constantly. Before long, I found myself all but stuck in the gluey insides of the coiled matter, all but dispersed there, and with a huge effort, I pulled away and ran out the child's ear. The brain is not the mind.

I lay uncoiled and suddenly afraid, suddenly alone. I realized that I had never been alone for any time at all. School to home was followed by school to the Reeds', the bakery, then Del and the Beausoleils, the bank, the kids, the church, the garden club. Even in death I was focused on people: visiting Larissa, checking up on various bank people, and of course my investigators and the ones who joined them later. I'd even gone to the graveyard, wondering why I was alone, even though the town had its ordinary roster of the dead. I had wanted to get a chance at Harmon and Addie, to tell them all the things I had done in spite of them—even the language I used. I suppose that with the dissolution of their bodies, the dead lose interest in a world in which they have no way of touching or tasting or smelling, and where vision and hearing work as a kind of skill remembered, almost metaphoric. If a person has been misunderstood or her motives misinterpreted, listening to the betrayers is too painful to bear. Better to fall backward into the ground where the dissolving body lies and to take refuge in the protecting cage of bones. One of the more recent dead told me this before he pulled away from the tree he was inhabiting and watered into the air insubstantial, absent. It was Delorme, the letter carrier we used to see at the bank, a boy again, the way he remembered himself. He slipped by and was gone and I was—I am—alone.

I had to do something. Fury is no stranger to this neuro-anatomy of mine. I can feel rage's tightness throughout my one-time-body. I have to tell the authorities everything—where the money is, why I took it—how what I did was a much-deserved revenge. Now and then I'd been up with Pastor Fearing and his lovely wife, Cheryl, a bitch on wheels. It had been amusing to watch him preach peace in church when he never had any at home. She denies him sex and she denies him the children he wants. She uses his Christianity against him. There would be more sympathy for him if his congregation knew.

Fearing does pray and he means it. He perceives a God I don't. Maybe because of that, I decided to go in to him in some way and tell him what I have done and where the money is and make him know what to tell the wolves that are gathering around my family.

I flowed up the hill to the church and past it to the parsonage. He was there, sitting in the shade made by his wicker chair's basket top, reading a mystery. Beside him was a little table with a glass of iced tea medicated with a little liquor. It seemed to smell gassy. For a moment, I hung in the air thirty feet away, taking in the sight. Fearing is a busy man and I still harbor a little anger for his trying to get the girls to give up my house to the church while they were weakened with the shock of my death. The sight of this sun-sated leisure stopped me and I was struck dumb with the sudden blow of my losses. Remember how tired I was after a stretch in the garden, and how I would come into the house, relishing its coolness, and how I would wash my hands in the cool water, all but groaning with pleasure as the water eased my fingers, hot and sweaty with work. Remember how good the first cup of morning coffee tasted and looking out the window to what kind of a day it was. Remember lying in the bathtub, the hot water pulling ease all my body long. Remember the taste of grapes, their texture in the mouth.

I began to cry. It was a strange, unsatisfactory series of mewing sounds. It had been years since I cried, the last time at Dr. Bendixen's funeral, with Del gone for the last time and me all alone with Addie and Harmon.

Cheryl walked out and went past Fearing without a look or a word. He had glanced up and nodded to her. It occurred to me that she might be a better candidate for my intrusion; we are both good haters. Garden club gossip had it that her disappointment was because she had expected much higher placements for him. She wanted LA; she got Topeka. She wanted Scarsdale; she got Gold Flume, Colorado, and while we are now sophisticated and gentrified with wealthy vacationers, the steady population consists of people like me. Cheryl disappeared behind the corner of the parsonage and we heard the car start.

I came close and pulled myself out long, thin as a wire, and threaded myself in through Fearing's ear. This exercise, which I had done only twice before, has taught me an awe about our workings. I've felt the webs of veins and the arteries with their valve-doors sliding shut to keep the urgent blood from its importunity. I've looked into the eye and seen a series of highways and roads running north to south and a hub busy as a city with flows of blood- what magic there is. Here I am in a pagan city inside a Christian pastor. I need to find where the thoughts are kept or generated and to go past the fittings and the flows all in the dark.

This worked no better with Fearing than it had done with the child. By the time I realized that there was no way in, I was nearly destroyed myself, pulled apart in the waves of his living. It took me the rest of the day to re-form myself after he expelled me in a sneeze.

So there was no way. All those reports over the centuries of people hearing the voices that gave them impetus are of another order than what I can command or receive. The brain of the FBI's most intuitive agent is no closer than the five-year-old I tried. And where I can go in and make the clever agents find, and in finding understand that I did what I needed to do—I and not my precious daughters or my gifted Mark or my wounded Gary, nor my wide-awake young granddaughter or my still self-enwrapped grandsons—I can't leave them now. I've stayed away from them out of respect. Now, I have to follow them to spy on them, and find a way to save them.

TWENTY-THREE
ARLIE

I WISH WE COULD HAVE gone to Portland with Karen and Mark—maybe if we had all been able to go, we would have visited Mark's cousins and gone camping, renting what we needed, and gotten away from our minds and our fears for a while. Gary came home with a fistful of prescriptions, but I'm sure he knows that what he's suffering from is a form of grief, not the grief that's open to the tears that ease a person but a grief all clouded with rage and fear. We are being investigated. For what? Protestations are met with suspicion. Our lives are being picked apart to find what? Checks and credit-card entries to forgotten people and places, highlighted and made much of.

"Two hundred dollars. And you don't remember to whom?"

Was it for the chair I had fixed? Was it for swimming lessons? I sometimes forget to fill in the *for* line on the checks I write and there's no space on the credit card account to jog my memory, and which, after I pay the bill, I don't keep anyway, or didn't.

I think Karen and Mark made a mistake, taking the kids to Portland. When they got back they got Bonnie Lewis to take them over to her house, which Jenny resented. Jenny wanted to stay home, guarding what hadn't been taken, and in the security of her own bed. She protested long and loud about there being no need for Bonnie. I've decided to include the kids in everything. They're younger than Karen's are—Luke's only nine, but they know there's trouble. I think knowing something— even when it's as bad as that Grandma whom they loved is dead and can't defend herself and is being accused of doing something awful—is better than seeing strangers coming through the house, taking things and questioning us, and having neighbors stare and whisper. We called Karen and Mark in Portland and asked if we could get all the kids together, Jenny and Evan along with our three, and tell them everything. We convinced them. I think Karen and Mark had suffered much more than we had—the elder daughter, the one with the husband who owns three buildings in town, she was the one to watch.

Gary's home computer was taken also, of course, and mine, but Gary can still go to work and so can I.

Even Dan, he's only six, knew about the mess, in some dim way, the tension, and his dad's sickness. He hadn't been around when our house was searched, but he had sensed it all with his kid's ability to feel tremors in his landscape.

When Karen, Mark, and the kids came back, we took them all up to the campground that the town had put in at the end of Mom's River Walk, now ten years old. It had recently been spaced with lay-bys for benches. The Feds wanted to know where Mom had gotten the money for that walk, and we'd been able to prove that the idea and energy had been hers, but that the money had come from the garden club's sales of seeds and bulbs and from the proceeds of yard and bake sales. The walk was Mom's crown. The campground was small, under an acre, but with bear-proof waste containers and two composting toilets set back against the side of the hill.

We set out the picnic and saw, as we ate, how restrained everyone was. The usual bitching and who-hit-whom among the kids was mercifully dampened, yet the reason wasn't peace but anxiety, and the growing mystery of something troubling the adults, the foundations of their lives. So we ate, chicken sandwiches, my chocolate cake, the half I had frozen from Michelle's birthday, corn chips, pickles—no fires, it being August, and so no marshmallows, but a concoction Jenny and Michelle had made up of apples, sliced and then layered with peanut butter, cream cheese, and slivered dates between the slices. The apple slices always tended to slide on the peanut butter and cheese and make a mess that never failed to delight every kid, until now.

I don't think I ever worked so hard to explain something to five kids as I did at that sour picnic. "What did Grandma do? What do they say she did?" "Why was what Grandma did supposed to hurt us?" "Did Grandma know it was going to hurt us?" "Were those men bad, who came to the house?" "Are we bad?"

Gary told me later that he thought he had made a botch of it. His own anguish came through under the dry, objective telling of what facts we had. "We don't know what Grandma did. A lot of money was missing from the bank and you all know that Grandma worked there for a long time. Those men were trying to find out what did happen and where the money was. Yes, Jenny, they took all our computers, even yours, to see if there was any record of where the money might be. When they find there's no money that there shouldn't be, that they made a mistake, they'll give the computers back and everything will go back to the way it was."

I love my niece. Jenny is bright and full of colors and sounds—easy glum, easy glow. We all worried more about what she would suffer than we did about the other kids who are younger and less tender.

A week went by and our house, always noisy with friends and fights over who left the top off the toothpaste, was hushed, more hushed than it had been for Mom's funeral. With the computers gone, Gary couldn't do any work at home and spent most of his time up at the ski area. The work is more intense in the summer than it is during the season. People must have been ribbing him, but I don't think they believed for a minute that he had any of that damned money, and for some reason this got to him more than if he had it in that famous Swiss bank account.

"Don't they think I have the IQ?" he shouted at me. "Do they see me as a good-natured slob?"

I was shocked. "Why should honesty be mistaken for stupidity?"

"It is," he said, and two days later he was home from the area late, and the day after that wasn't home at all.

I called the manager of the area, who told me that Gary had left early, saying that he had business in Aureole and asking for the vacation time he had coming. I called friends, and the hospital in Aureole and, later, the police. No word. Gary is a very moderate drinker, but the situation isn't moderate and we were all lost in a new landscape with roads never explored before. My mind pictured him in a dive in Aureole, drinking.

Days passed. Then a week. We were very suddenly changed, amputated. The pay for my job, which had been used for vacations and luxuries, wasn't enough to cover the realities of food and utilities and the incidentals of home. We had bought a new car. There were payments. We had a cleaning lady who wept when I told her I couldn't keep paying her. "You're good people," she said, "I hate what happened." Is happening, I thought, is going on like a train wreck, each connected car after car going downhill to join the calamity at the bottom of the ravine, all in slow motion.

Gary sent a letter: I'm near Deming, New Mexico, working at a Walmart and living with some guys in a cabin. I can't come back, yet. I always felt like an imposter, the family, the job. You know I never graduated engineering school the way I said I did. The ski area never checked. I learned the job and I did it. I thought I had a real family, but I'm fake and it's fake and the foundation of it is a lie. This job I have now is what I was raised to do, and who I was raised to be. I love you and the kids and I might be able to find my way back to you some way, but not in Gold Flume, not with a false life and false identity. It seemed worth it, Mom and my belonging—town, house, job, family, in-laws, car—all someone else's life. Forgive me.

Whatever I had known about Gary, his insecurity, his very quiet way of slipping through life, I hadn't known that he hadn't graduated engineering school. His small deception explained a lot that puzzled me. He almost never spoke of his past—I knew that he had been a foster kid, but he never told me how many of those homes he had been in, or where, or for how long. College? Mentioned, but not told about. There were none of the tales of mishap or adventure that people keep to polish and tell a group of friends out for an evening, or kids over Sunday breakfast. Clear emotions have a kind of ring to them. They're there to be understood. The clamor, the doubled and trebled emotions are a bad chord, grating and dissonant. The letter was shaking in my hand.

A week later, he was back, but he was someone else, a blurred copy.

"I thought about my being a fake," he said, "and I thought about Lily. I am, she was, but you and the kids aren't fakes, and since you didn't marry me because I was an engineer, I want to take the true parts of myself and try again."

"I think it's time to leave here," I said. "The kids have been having it rough, being picked on. Cheryl Fearing happened to us, Karen and me at the mall, shopping. She was bitchy. Luther Hayes has left and there has been almost a run on the bank. People are afraid for their money."

"Where would we go?"

"Somewhere in the western hemisphere," I said.

"Very helpful."

"I like small-town life," I said. "I like Colorado. We could go to Gunnison or Glenwood Springs, to Salida, to Grand Junction—"

"No more faking."

"What were you faking? You've been working as an engineer for ten years, getting respect for what you've done."

"I can't be a fake."

"Then what would you want to be doing?"

"I don't know—I'd have to see what's available where we go. How much money do we have?"

"We'd sell this house and hope not to take too big of a loss on it. I'd work it through the office and get Marilyn to show it for us. Last year we'd have gotten flak from the kids. They used to love being here. Now—we, now—"

"It was nice, though, Mark and Karen, their kids, ours, and…"

He couldn't say Lily's name. "I think Mark is more invested here than we are. Karen wouldn't mind moving. Jenny would want to."

"Get us a place," Gary said. "Get us a place to be."

TWENTY-FOUR
JENNY

SCHOOL STARTED, MY LAST YEAR in middle school, thank God. The new school opened in Callan three years ago when I first went. The teachers made a big deal out of how this was a new start and there shouldn't be cliques here and how we should all get along and focus on our education so we could get into college and not be pulled back by the stupid decisions we made when we were kids. Lots of luck. Kimberly, Brittany, Samantha, and Ariel—the same top girls did the same top things. The boys were as stupid as ever. I'm living past it all. I got dragged into the top clique a couple of times because I'm smart and some of the kids want to copy my homework. Brittany got pregnant, which she should be, because she was doing it with half the mouth-breathers that ride home with us on the bus.

I want to be a writer. They have great lives. They're famous, but not like the celebrities who have screaming fans and hate mail and the stuff you read at the checkout that show pictures of them when they look bad just to bring them down and make readers gawk and laugh. Writers get to hang out with celebrities but not have to be them.

When I get to be a famous writer, I'll tell how cruel people are, especially girls, to your face and behind your back.

The racket now is about Gran. I loved her; I still do. I always will. She was good to all of us, but not like the grandmas on TV or some of them of kids I know—sweet and always baking cookies. My gran was dignified. She didn't smile as much as other grandmas are supposed to do. When you did something wrong, she would tell you, but in a way that made you feel okay after you fixed it, or stopped doing it, and when you were acting right, she let you know in a way I still can't figure out. I admire her—I think that's what I feel. I'm proud of her, but I'm not supposed to feel that way because people say she stole money from the bank.

Which is what everyone says, and the girls laugh at me because of. This has made a line in my life and in all our lives—mine and Evan's and Michelle's and Luke's.

Probably not in Dan's, though, because he's only six and his life will all be on this side of the line.

The line is before people found out about the money, and after.

We were pretty big in town, before. The day she died, they had a big party for Gran. Lots of people retire from work, but people told me that no one but Gran ever had a party like that. I was there in a new dress—no pants, please—and Mom and Dad and Aunt Arlie and Uncle Gary and a huge cake and all the bank people.

Then she died, and there was the funeral and the whole town was at Gran's church, the mayor and the people from the bank and the garden club. I wrote that speech and gave it and people said it was good. People told a lot about her that I didn't know. Up at the cemetery there was a big crowd, too. None of us knew that there was going to be that before-and-after line, one that someone was beginning to draw that day.

The kids in school laugh at us. Luke and Evan say they hate to go to school now, because everyone teases them and trips them up when they are walking up to the board or during recess. Then they have to fight whoever it was, and you can't fight the whole school. Sometimes the teachers see these things happening and they stand there and say nothing. Mrs. Bergson said, "Really, dear, you can't blame them."

But I can. Dad told me that no one in town lost money. The bank is insured, he said, which means that whatever Gran took, if she really took anything, the company will pay it back. I don't understand how that works. I don't know how much money Gran is supposed to have taken, either. No one seems to know, so I've heard it was a million, two million, ten million—except that it's funny, because Gran wasn't a rich person. When we went to Portland to visit our cousins, they had a great time introducing us to electricity and running water in their home, because we come from a small town, and probably don't have those things. Then we had to tell them that four movie stars have built houses between Gold Flume and Callan and football stars and foreign rich people live between Callan and Bluebank and send their kids to school with us, sometimes. That means I know what rich people have. When Yaya Sastromojojo goes back to Indonesia for vacations, she goes to LA in a private plane and yes, we have an airport in the Valley, and a helipad. The only reason Gran had a car was because the grocery and hardware stores moved out of town and out to the mall near Callan. She drives—she drove—there every other week and up to see Aunt Arlie and her family, and to do her charity work with the old people, visiting them. I'll bet that car has no more than five hundred miles on it. Jewelry? Mom gave it to

Michelle and me after Gran died. There were some pins, two rings, and two necklaces. Where did she get all those pearls, that silver and gold? Dad. Dad, and Uncle Gary, for her birthdays and Christmas. I saw her get some of them myself. I found out—what's the worst thing? I think the worst thing is injustice, when you're blamed for something you didn't do, or when you have lies told about you. You want to yell how it isn't fair. You start dreaming up things to make people see what's true. I wrote scenes in my notebook where Gran comes back and kills the kids who teased Evan and Luke in school, and then, when their parents come crying to us, tells them that she will bring them back to life if they never say another bad thing about her. Another scene is where Gran shows that someone has told a big lie about her and set up a plan against her at the bank and carried it out with all the rest of the bank officials because they were lazy and didn't care.

Pastor Fearing came to our house. We got sent upstairs. I came halfway down to a spot we often stayed at, Evan and me, to sit and listen in on plans, or when the parents were arguing. You can tell where we sat because the banister has lots of scratches down near where the stair carpet is. Aunt Karen and Uncle Mark came. I never understood what Raise the Roof meant, but I do now. I have grown up thinking it was some boring thing, church donations or a special fund, but when I heard those voices—Evan was in his room playing with some card tricks—I was sure it wasn't about any fund.

I hadn't been in on the start of the conversation, but it seemed like Pastor Fearing wanted Gran's house. At first I thought that was too wild and far out an idea to be true, but it was true, and he was there saying things like how *they* would take the house, they being the government because of the money, and if our family gave up the house now, before any charges were filed, and it was for charity… Dad, who is a lawyer, said right away that what the family decided to do or not do would be decided by its members and not by what an outsider proposed, who was, in fact, insinuating himself for the benefit of his own interests.

I loved the words he said. I repeated them three or four times, missing more of the conversation—"there he was, insinuating himself for the benefit of his own interests"—I want to save that idea and words for some special moment when it will fit in my writing like the little ball in the roulette machine.

There were other things people said with louder voices, until I thought the roof would move off the house, pushed up by the sounds they were making. Pastor left, but I was surprised that the argument went on, as if he hadn't left at all. It blew hotter, about Gran, but then dragging in stuff that happened years ago. I thought of corn popping, anger at Gran, at each other, the uncles and the aunts and my parents; Mom and Aunt Arlie crying, crying and yelling.

Parents' yelling isn't like anyone else's, not like ours. Kids yell about nothing and parents' yelling shakes the world. We so seldom heard it that when it came, it made a big statement to us. There was something more than anger in their shouting and the memories they threw at each other. These were things they had covered up for years and suddenly woke up again in their shouting.

Gran did steal the money. I sat there on the steps, clinging to the bottom of one of the banister rungs that was sticky with years of kid-fingered food, years of kids sitting here, listening to grown-ups deciding things. I knew that was true so suddenly and so altogether that I almost yelled myself. Knowing that explained everything: those hard, angry men coming to take everyone's computers, the laughing of the kids in school, the anger of Uncle Gary and Aunt Arlie at Mom and Dad, and Mom and Dad at each other. And you could believe it, too, the whole story.

Nobody will ever forget this, not Gold Flume or Callan or Bluebank or Granite City, not the whole Valley. What was safe and friendly will be gone and friends and strangers will point to us and wonder where the money is.

Where is it? We can look all day and all night and I know we don't have it; at least I don't think we have it. If we did, wouldn't we have cars and boats and vacations and private school for all of us kids? I know Dad is important in town. He goes to lots of meetings and makes lots of decisions. He's on the boards of things. I don't really know how rich we are. I know we don't have what people think we have...now.

Something awful has happened to me. We play volleyball in phys ed. I've been missing the ball when I go for it—not by an inch, I miss by a foot...feet. I trip on curbs. I misjudge distances—badly. The gym teacher told me I needed to get my eyes checked and that I may need glasses, but I think I can see okay. Mom says it's growing and that I don't have my full body that I can get used to, because it keeps changing, but this is something else, something I'm afraid of. I often get dizzy and have a nauseated feeling. It's all...everything is out of control.

Evan used to chatter. Now he comes home and goes right to the PlayStation. Dad got him that while the authorities were studying his old one. He stays on it all day playing those games, the ones you can play for free.

TWENTY-FIVE
LARISSA

OF COURSE IT WAS A shock to everyone—and after all we had done for her. There's something more obscene and embarrassing about old people involved in crime than there is about young ones. Everyone asks me, being an Ellie and the only one still alive—you can't count Lowayne, of course, who's never quite focusing on you when you are talking, and now so brain-pickled it's a wonder she doesn't lose herself in her own house—to explain her, to summon up the memories of our girl- and young-womanhood. I've been asked by all kinds of people, new acquaintances and old friends, what she was like. Did I know she had these propensities?

Because of this curiosity, I wasn't surprised when the *Ute River Voice* and then the *Denver Post* asked me for an interview. The *Post's* article was a big disappointment—a three-hour meeting that resulted in a column that gave little more than Lily's name and age and what she'd done and that she had committed suicide before any investigation had begun. I could have given those facts over the phone instead of being bothered for three hours in an afternoon.

The *Ute River Voice*, a smaller paper of course, sent its woman—girl, really, and I was pleasantly surprised at the skill she used. Of course, a story like mine doesn't happen every day. The girl seemed moved to hear about how we had been chosen in a kind of random move, given the idea of being Ellies, and how that meant that we had managed to all but save Lily's life after her parents died. Of course, by this time, no one remembers them, feeble-minded, both of them, working that charity job at a grocery that closed fifty years ago and no sign of which remains in our new downtown. She didn't quote me on that, but wrote "humble people." I remembered their name: Higgins. I told her how my father had taken Lily in when the two of them died, and how LuAnne had died just about then, and so how the Reeds gave her a home, so that she might replace—she looked at me with a strange expression when I said replace—but I said that LuAnne had been bigger and her clothes had not fit on Lily at first—but that Lily had grown into them. Then I told her to remember that those were the war years—

World War II. People didn't have ration stamps to throw away or money, either. I told her about Lily's going to work at the bakery, and that the Reeds hadn't been all that happy about it, and then how Lily had worked her wiles on Del Beausoleil so that he had to marry her. When I said "worked her wiles" I saw the girl's eyebrows go up. I suppose the phrase isn't used much anymore. All right, I'm not up on the latest in how people tell things, like the "I'm like wow" the grandkids use. Don't you think Del Beausoleil could have done better than little Lily Higgins? Why didn't he? They were rich, as town-rich went in those days. There were four big houses in town, left over from the big places the railroad men and mine owners used for vacations, winter sports and summer fishing in the 1880s and 1890s when Gold Flume was someplace. Grandchildren, heirs, lived in one of the houses; one had been turned into a town library; one, near the river, was derelict, a haunted house the kids fantasized about...I did, too, as a child.

The Beausoleils were new in town, only a generation in that house that was right up the street from the center of town, a landmark. Addie and Harmon kept the outside spruce-looking. Del used to take those front steps three at a time, I remember, in and out so easily. He had been an army hero during the war, Korea, that is. He had medals. After the war he had stayed away. I forget why, and then we heard he had gone to California, but in 1958 he was back home. Maybe he had been in California to be a movie star. He certainly had the looks for it, and that sauntering walk…strength coiled, a walk easy because of his perfect confidence in his power.

And who, of all the girls glued to front windows or moving down streets on made-up errands? Lily.

I think she ruined him. I don't know how. She wasn't demanding clothes or a rich life. I think it must have been that she needed security. The Reeds weren't happy with her. She saw Del and that big house and maybe she decided to lie down for him and then got up, dusted herself off, and yelled "pregnant." And guess what: it was all a terrible mistake. I've heard that one before, and of course by the time the wedding bells were ringing the pregnancy was real.

I could see the reporter begin to be restless, shifting her eyes. She wanted to know about Lily's work at the bank. I had to tell her that the truth was that none of us thought she was smart enough to do all that, twenty or thirty years of stealing and covering it up, to do what they say she did. The Lily Beausoleil I knew was no genius. She seldom said a word, and when she did, it was about the garden club. She didn't rave on her grandkids; I'll give her that. Quiet. She was quiet.

Another thing I'll give her, and that was that she raised those girls and sent them both to college, and it was after Harmon and Addie died and we found out that the house was all they had. Maybe that's why she stole the money. The girls had college and married well, and, to all our surprise, stayed in town. Mine are in Boston, Phoenix, and San Diego. The reporter asked me what emotion I felt—Lily's deceiving us all like that. Surprise, I think, like a lost kitten you'd pick up to save it from an owl, and the kitten bares its teeth and scratches and bites you, and jumps away. We saved her. Didn't she understand that?

TWENTY-SIX
LOWAYNE

WHEN YOU KNOW THAT YOU can get to a case of rye in your cellar and another one in the pantry, and there's a liquor store down the block anyway, you don't have to drink as much as you did when the certainty wasn't there. It's the Thou Shalt Not that assures you that Thou Shalt. Charlie did that for us. When we was flush, way back in the years, he laid in cases of Scotch for him and gin for me and rye for both of us.

So here comes this reporter and asks can she come in and talk about Lily. Sure. She tells me she has been to see Larissa, and was intrigued, she said, intrigued about how we got to be the Ellies and have it all work like it did. I told her it wasn't no mystery. Aren't families like that? A bunch of people chosen by other people who you're supposed to love and be with? We didn't fit, us Ellies, but until we were grown we did look out for each other some, and being an Ellie gave at least three of us a name and a place.

LuAnne was quiet as a mouse in sneakers, so polite and so careful you wanted to hit her sometimes, just to get a reaction. The boys would have done her in if not for us. She was an Ellie for three years until she died.

Then there was my reason: four brothers, four sisters—a crowd I could get lost in, and here I was, suddenly separate, chosen. That being chosen was better than cocaine, better than booze, for me. I loved being wild, but I guess it was because it made me stand out from all those other kids. None of our crowd—the wild ones—stayed here, only me, and because I'm a drunk they don't have no contact with me. My son, either, Charlie's and mine.

I don't know why I told the reporter all that, I just said it, a statement, and on and on and only realized later that I never said all of that to anyone before. When you're old, you get to say lots of things you never could say before. Your brain goes slack, along with everything else.

Larissa was the only one who didn't need to be an Ellie, but, thinking it over, it seems like she must have got her share of its good part, something like her being able to be Queen Elizabeth visiting her royal possessions in Swaziland. Then there was Lily. People will tell you how Town raised her after her folks died. They did, so she never got to say what dress she wanted to wear, what shoes, what food she got to eat. It's why she loved her job at the bakery—good choice—serving other people instead of being their project. Then there was the bad choice: Del. When I heard about all the bank business, I laughed. I laugh every time I think about it. What a way to turn things around, what a neat, sweet secret, all those years.

When I said that, the reporter looked at me like I had just dropped my drawers and mooned her. I had to tell her that gratitude gets old and that suffering may not make you better, but worse. The people who recommend it don't recommend it for themselves.

People say different, but in their saying they give themselves away. While the suffering is going on, you're hanging on to whatever's there, in the ocean of it. It ends, or your foot touches bottom at some time, and you pull to shore and pull yourself up on dry land and start over. All that takes every bit of energy you got. But soon, you're living and you get to thinking back and it seems like all that suffering and struggle has made you a little smarter than other people. You got behind the thing, deeper than they did. I been there. You think that stuff when you're really drunk, arrogant because you see deeper, you think, than ordinary people. I seen Blacks who have it: prisoners, veterans of one kind or another, not all of them, just the ones that need it.

The poor reporter girl went bleary-eyed on me. I started to laugh. I laughed at how Lily has put it over on the whole town and skipped out before the bills piled up. Who would think she'd pull off such a neat trick? I laughed until tears ran and my diaphragm was cramping and sore. The reporter—first chuckling a bit along with me the way someone's laughter draws you along with it—got scared. Her laughter went clacky with her nervousness and then stopped altogether. I had wet my pants a little.

She went away. I doubt she'd use any of what I told her in her article, and in any case I wouldn't be reading it. I don't get the *Voice*, which has only the news about three of the four towns in the Ute Valley and only if there's a super scandal is there anything but the wonderful revelations of people like Larissa, who give parties and donate and raise money with style shows.

Remembering gave me the oddest feeling, almost like causing the thing all over again, but this time, coming at it from another side, and so seeing it in a new way. Except for the good laugh I got and the good laugh I get when I think about Lily, I don't value it much, remembering. There are too many surprises. Even the dead can surprise you.

TWENTY-SEVEN
MIKE DAVIS

So it was just before ski season started when this place wakes up like there's nightlife, and just off downtown, and you could get there in five minutes and there's lots of places where you could get a drink. They'll serve you if you're six years old in the right ones, but you got to know. The only ones right in town are tight-ass and make you show your license. I have one fake one, anyway, that Herb made me. Most of the time it works. The thing is you don't want to use it unless the place is full and the attention is off of you because of lots of people wanting drinks.

Me and Tim and Joe Wall were walking up First three days ago and we seen the big house the old lady who stole all the money used to live in. Tim said he thought we could get in there and see what it was like.

Lots of rumors were going around and one was that the place had the money she stole and someone found out years ago and she killed them and put them in the attic and maybe two or three people over the years who disappeared because they found out about her stealing and she invited them up or something and then killed them. They would all be still there or in the cellar. There would be a trap door that the Feds didn't find. Joe said the Feds had been there looking for the money. It would be interesting to go in where the Feds were.

They have streetlights but only starting at the bottom for downtown. We got into the house that night. I have a sweet deal, because I can get out the back kitchen door after the folks go to bed, which is that their room is way on the other side of the house. I been using that since I was ten. Me and Joe met by the back of his place. He could have run a war and his ma and pa wouldn't have woke up because they both doped up every night on booze, which they buy from Tim's uncle, which is how we met Tim in the first place. Aside from that he was in school with us.

We got in the house easy because there was a cellar, which most of the houses around here don't have because of the rock you'd have to blast to make one. There was a window around back, all hid from the stores, which was a frame shop and a knitting place, both closed. Anyway, there were bushes that sucked up the sound we made getting in.

We had four flashlights and once we got in, we knew we didn't have to be super careful except when we were in rooms where there was windows looking out into the street. What a place. There was four staircases, four of them: one up from the cellar and two on the main floor, with a big one with a banister and one in the back, smaller, to the kitchen, which was like a hotel, all in tiles. We did the whole place. There was another staircase to the top floor. There was some furniture still in it, tables and chairs and beds upstairs, all in a mess because the place had been searched and no one had really been in after that to clean up what the FBI and them had gone into. The electricity was turned off and there was nothing in the food part of the place. The cabinets and the food closets was cleaned out, no dishes or silverware. I thought of taking something, but Tim said that unless I could sell it off the Valley, it would be stupid because people would know who it belonged to. We went up the big staircase that didn't have a carpet, which I thought rich houses all had because this creaked something awful, like broken bones all the way up. We stopped on the second floor and went through all the rooms, looking in the closets and opening the drawers the FBI had stuck their hands into back last month. I don't know why we thought we'd be smarter than they were, and smarter at night in the dark than they were during the day, but up through all the rooms and up to the third floor, we started to get mad, for a reason I can't remember now. The attic—no trapdoor up to it, real steps, and three good rooms along with the big attic place that had the trunks and stuff, was just a boring attic, nothing special. The lady had millions and no one knew where it was, and we knew it was in this house, so we started to knock on the walls for hollow places, or different-sounding places, anyway. Joe said we should think it out. If the secret hiding place was any good, it wouldn't be all but impossible to get to. It would be in a place you go to all the time. I laughed and said "the bathroom" and he gave me a poke in the head. Tim said he thought it would be in the library, behind all those books. She would know which ones and we should look for the ones that didn't look new.

We'd been walking up the stairs and down, being excited and intense the way you get at the beginning of a big adventure, but we was at this for maybe three hours, and all at once all three of us started to feel how cold it was. When we got to the library, it was cold, but while we was there, a wind came up—not a real big one, but enough for us to hear it outside and feel it inside, like around your ankles from the draft. Joe said it was from the window we broke. Anyway, it was freezing.

I'm no dummy. I run upstairs and get two old blankets we found in the bedrooms and took them down and we sat wrapped up in them to think. We had maybe three more hours before we had to get out but I said we could come back every night until we found the money.

Sitting, figuring made us colder in spite of the blankets and we thought—I thought—we could start a fire. There was a big fireplace in the library that had wood in it, and there was enough paper around the place—three copies of the *Voice* right there in a kind of rack beside the door. I went to the kitchen and found some matches, but by then, Tim yelled to me that he had found some by the fireplace—big long ones. That's how safe we felt, him yelling like that, and us going in and out with the flashlights—two of them was pretty faint by then.

We tore up the *Voice* and stuffed the papers around the wood that was in the fireplace and lit it. Joe had put the sort of stand that was in front of the fireplace away, and he fell over it with a huge clang and we laughed. The papers flared and went out and we put in more paper, all the copies of the *Voice* tore off, and before we lit it again, Tim said we should get some smaller wood or wooden stuff out of the kitchen. I had to piss and so did Joe, so we found a bathroom off the kitchen and used that, and took a roll of toilet paper that was there and unrolled lots of that, and a couple of wood chairs we broke, and stuck all of that in around the logs and lit that. For maybe two minutes, it looked like it was going out, and then we saw it was taking, way in back. Then there was a big fire, really big, but you couldn't be sure if it was the wood that was burning or the paper, and then there was a big *whoosh* and smoke and sparks started filling the room. We was choking and I saw little bits of fire, shreds hitting the floor where there was a big rug. There was a curtain, too. I yelled to Tim and Joe that we should go quick to the kitchen and get some water, but I started to cough so I ran out of there and felt someone with me, which was Joe. He got to the kitchen and was looking around for something like a pail or a dishpan we could fill up. We figured those little sparks could be put out if we had water. Joe was coughing and there was no water. I was thinking we needed to get back quicker than we were working. Back in the library Joe said there was a gizmo on the fireplace we should have fixed to get the fire to go up the chimney. "Hell of a time to tell me," I said. He said something back and soon we was yelling at each other.

There was so much smoke in there, we couldn't see, or even get in the room, but I once heard you should hit the floor, which I did, and that was smart, because I remembered where the window was, and if I could break it, the smoke would go out. We thought maybe Tim had gone somewhere. I found him on the floor near the window. There were bits of burning stuff all around. I was coughing, too, by then, and I couldn't find the place I thought the window was, but I did find it and as soon as I broke it I would pull Tim out, maybe out through the window.

I pulled my sweater over my head and got to my knees and stood up. I had a knife in my pocket and I took that out and as hard as I could, I slammed it against the window. The window broke.

Then—and I hardly had time to be surprised—it was all fire. I had thought I would breathe air because of being at the window, but I breathed fire and I heard the roar of it all around. I tried to breathe out, but I couldn't, and it was all too hot and too late, a terrible sound, high as the highest wire of pain which was me and then…no then.

Then I was standing with Joe and Tim watching firemen running with hoses to the house, and we were in a crowd of people in nightclothes. The house was a torch. Joe and Tim wanted to go back to their bodies, now that fire wouldn't hurt them. They both went back inside. I felt the pull too, but doesn't everyone want to get the feeling of being without a body? It's true that standing in a crowd like I was, people tended to push together and I got…scattered, sort of, and it was hard to reconnect my trailings. Still—I used to think of going home with a girl and being invisible and watching her undress all the way, and getting into bed with her, invisible, and licking her boobs and…except I figured out she'd start to scream and they'd catch me by throwing flour or paint or something that would show my body.

A girl was right next to me. I slid in through her sleeve and spread out, body to body. There was nothing. I poured out past her boobs, waist, twat, everything I wanted so bad for so long, trying to get, even girls I didn't like that much. I tried rubbing myself right there, watching the house burn, standing next to everyone… nothing. I raised myself up above everybody to look over them. If I couldn't smell or feel… There was just the faintest feeling, something I remembered, I think. Then I got surprised. Shouldn't I be missing my folks? Shouldn't I be going back to see them, to sympathize with them as they got the news? Maybe Dad wouldn't be all that sad to see me go. We've been biting each other since I was twelve. Mom—I want gone from the whole family thing. One time up to now, I thought it would be great to fly around and go in people's houses or stores, snitch candy, and get booze and food and watches, but now there's no hungry and no sleeping and no way to drink. I felt a pull back into the house. The roof was burning. Soon I thought it would collapse into the house and then I wouldn't find my body. I began to pour forward into the flames but there was no heat for me. The library had been blocked by burning parts of the house fallen in there. It took me a long time to find my body, not as burned as I thought it would be because I had been in some kind of backdraft place under the window when the blast went through there.

There it was. I slid in. Tim was there and so was Joe, who I passed while I was looking for my body. There was something peaceful about sliding into it. I pulled the body around me. It fit. I knew I could free myself when I wanted to, but it felt good there. It felt right. We stayed. There was too much noise from the fire to talk.

TWENTY-EIGHT
LILY

I was lying curled up in a space between the chimney and an air vent at the town hall roof, a space I now inhabit as home. Nothing is as empty as somewhere that buzzes with people and action during the day and is deserted at night. I often flow in through the open door of the last person to leave for the day, comforting myself with the ordinary signs of living, the simple human presence. I flow up through the vent and lie here looking at the stars. Summer has become winter; the sun didn't burn me and the frost and falls of snow are not cold against my body. Only my memory evokes their differences.

There was a noise and people running. I looked over the slope of the roof and saw people heading for the firehouse, and there was the smell of fire as I remembered it. I saw the trucks going up First Street so I slid off the roof and floated down to the bed of hoses in the back of a pumper truck that was heading up the hill.

It was the house on fire, Addie and Harmon's house where I had lived my life, and it was spitting flame out of the downstairs windows. Neighbors from the back street had been alerted and were standing, watching, and the wives and kids of the firemen coming up to see this dramatic blaze.

The house was a loss. Firemen began to spray all around it to keep the flames and sparks from igniting the bushes and trees, only two, now, that could ignite the surrounding structures. Standing in the crowd, all faces but his reflecting the light of the fire, I saw a shadow-boy, one newly dead. He saw me and tried to come toward me, but he wasn't used to flowing so he began to roll in the air. He carried the smell of the fire, the little villain. At last, he stilled, detached himself from the crowd, slid by me, and tottered clumsily back into the fire.

Everyone was eager, straining to see and being pushed away by the fire chief. How avid and intent they looked, standing in their nightclothes, outfits they would ordinarily have been ashamed to show, warmed on this icy night by the flames that were eating my children's inheritance. I always hated the place, and it had surprised me to learn how much they all loved it. The land was still there, commercially valuable for another boutique, another gallery featuring smears of paint, another store carrying artisanal olive oil and sixteen kinds of artisanal salt. How elegant, to accept only this or that kind of salt.

* * * * *

My FBI cheering section is gone. They left after their searches of the houses and families I hadn't visited until their disruption by the wrong-headed law. I visited this morning. Jenny looks at her parents with doubt. The kids ask questions and have nightmares. Their youths will be impaled on the horns of my guilt or innocence. Where's the money? How could I have stolen it and hidden it and why? I knew a bank auditor or FBI man would ask these questions from the cool and level landscape of forensic accounting. Jenny's questions are anything but cool. They are dark with confusion and fear. Who was her grandma? Who can be trusted or loved? If Gran is innocent, why is the government pursuing her? Why is it suspecting us?

I remember how intent she was, asking me about my people. Did they grow up in Gold Flume—what were they like? I got away by pushing the years back a little—I was small when they died—I don't remember—Higgins. English, probably. There was one assignment in school about forebears. I never knew my mother's maiden name. I made one up—Levin, after the character in *Anna Karenina*. I sent Jenny to the town records about Addie and Harmon. Addie's father had been a boy soldier, imprisoned at Andersonville. That was interest enough.

I can't answer her. I have tried, screaming into the ears of everyone who could help, and no one has heard me. It's too painful to stay. The house is gone, but there will be plenty of money from the land—a prime site. Commercial zoning has been moving up that street for a decade and soon no one will remember the big old dinosaur that was there before. I've been liberated from that house at last. I'd tried all these years to blur and then to remove every trace of the Beausoleils—smell, sight, touch. I've worked my erasure with paint and paper, with new furniture, piece by careful piece, and if a dusty, fumy couch stood against a wall, a new table would go there, or a bookcase. Light and airy has replaced dark and pretentious in every room. Still, no matter how a corpse is dressed, it's still a corpse.

I saw the three boys die with the house. I was thinking they might—we might—together—but two of them after only few moments dove back into their bodies and turned themselves off. The third tried a move and failed, and joined his friends. What's the matter with youth these days—no courage, no imagination.

I left the fire and drifted back up to my perch under the eaves. Where did I want to go? I had no interest in staying where I was. Ordinary life was fading. How invested I had been in the reality of my senses—taste, smell, touch. There was no sleeping now and no waking. The people I care for deserve their freedom. I used to hear people say, "My dad is up in heaven, looking down at me," and "My mom is with me all the time." Do they really want that? Would those aging children want their idealized dead aware of their marital spats, banal exchanges, their pettiness, bitter moments, bathroom visits? Even famous and fascinating lives are nine-tenths commonplace. If that's so for my children and grandchildren, how much less interest do I have in any of the residents of this town I hate?

I was realizing these things and I decided to die. Much of the time when I was a physical weight in the world, I lived in expectation of very simple, small things: the waking of my garden, the burger-and-fry platter at LaForge where I took Jenny once a month. She would always agonize her way down the huge menu and wonder why I always had the same thing.

Burger and fries was the only link to my past that I allowed to creep into my carefully constructed present. Twice, Dr. Bendixen took me to the Two Freds for burgers and fries when I stayed with them, before the Reeds got me. I had been used to eating whatever was in the dented cans Mami and Papi brought home from

Henderson's Market. The lunch I had with him had been a revelation.

I looked forward to book club, to certain TV shows, to a new blouse, to an open window in my bedroom all summer. It turns out that small, very small, pleasures gather into a life that lifts them into something greater than their origins. I've been thinking a lot about pride lately. There hasn't been much more to think about. My point of pride turns out to be my vote against the garden club's plan to compete in local flower shows that would end in state and national competitions. How did I know that I would hate doing that? Why wouldn't a ragged kid who didn't know what an ivy plant was not want to knock the wind out of some judges? I saw why not on TV at the dog shows and car and horse shows they broadcast—the tight faces, the fisted hands, held behind backs. Not for me. We compromised by putting up the hanging baskets on Miner Street and creating the walk by the river. More than one club member ground her dentures when Town decided to name the walk for me. I see they've taken that plaque down.

House burned, garden trodden down by fire equipment and boots. Where did I want to be? Not where I was buried. I wanted to go home. I wanted to go to the Hungry Mother and lie down flat against the wind and let it take me there.

The Hungry Mother looks west and is, as it has always been, a place of hard terrain. Now, with the new technology, anyone can build almost anywhere, and it won't be long before that mountain is platted and buildings put on it, bought and sold for huge McMansions whose foundations will be blasted through the granite and quartz of these mountains. The place where Mami and Papi lived will be so reconfigured that no one, not even I, who was born there, would be able to remember how it was.

The people searching for the money have all my history before them, just as everyone in town did: orphan, unlucky bride, lucky widow with big house. It was all there, at the beginning, and no one looked.

So far, the Hungry Mother is the same as it was, minus our shack. Its terrain has kept it safe for now. On my sixtieth birthday, I walked up there to where I thought our cabin had been. I went with a pickaxe to try to find some bit of Mami and Papi, a rag of their clothing, a pan, a fragment of a bedstead, or a shard of the bowl we washed in. Nothing was where I dug. Then I realized that cabin, people, things had all been swept down-mountain, crushed, broken, separated, pounded apart. Later, everything must have been hauled away when the dirt road was made into a two-lane and then a four-lane and the Ute channeled. The avalanche had cleared the mountain's face except for up-thrust rock. Over the years young saplings had ventured out on its small pockets of blown soil. They had cleaved the lamina that had been laid down in the formation of these mountains, when giant lizards with telescoping heads had walked here. The lizard tracks are here now, but not my Mami and Papi.

What I did, then, was to find exactly where the house had been. I did this by lining the whole landscape out with all the other signs and landmarks I had learned standing at our open door on nights of my childhood. Then I used the pick and began to score the rock, which split. I worked until I had made a hole, widened by my pulling up loose rock slabs. I put into the hole a bracelet I had made with painted, rolled-up pieces of paper. The idea had come from a craft book for children. I covered up the hole with a slab of rock.

The first important addition to the bracelet in the hole was a pounded flat slab of two ounces of twenty-four-carat gold. I deepened the hole in 1975 and again in 1988 and yet again in 1998, a year ago, when I found the slab I used to cover the hole almost too heavy for me to move any more. By that time there were seven gold bars in the memorial representing my fortune, larger or smaller depending on the price of gold. It symbolized everything I had been given by the town that refused to remember the names of my Mami and my Papi: Ernestine Higgins, Marshall Higgins. Gold, pure gold, is soft. It can be chiseled easily.

I used a tool, one I got from a dentist years before, a throwaway that had been broken on one end, used to scrape the plaque from teeth. On each of those gold bars are the names I carved there. I never knew the names of any brothers or sisters they might have had, their parents, their aunts or uncles. As runaways they had fled from more than the institution where they had met. They lived in perpetual fear of being found and returned, although the place in which they had been imprisoned had long since closed its doors. I never knew which state it had been in. I do know that they had left with no money and had walked for days, perhaps for weeks, eating from garbage cans at the backs of restaurants and sleeping in deserted buildings or unlocked automobiles. This I had wormed out of Mami as we washed floors or made beds or worked together shoring up the sagging back end of the cabin or at the wash line, word by word, bit by bit.

They seemed to have no memories that provided dimension or context. In the institution, there a man named Secombe, who was cruel, and a man named Havercroft, who was kind and with whom they tried to stay close when Secombe was there. That was all I could elicit from either of them in our years together, that and the fear, always, that they might be caught and punished and returned to their separate wards, that the world, which they did not understand, was judging them and had to be kept mollified at all costs.

Now, they are memorialized by what I have figured to be three million five hundred thousand eight hundred sixty-six dollars in twenty-four-carat gold, their names on every bar, buried in rock on the site of their cabin and providing me a thumb in the eye of the town that had condescended to them and been sanctimonious to their daughter. Why did I assume that the people of today would be any brighter than the ones I encountered in my youth? Their arrogance has increased but not their intelligence or their patience or their capacity for thought.

My needs have caused misery to my family, the people I loved. I didn't think the blow would fall so heavily on them, or that I would be unable to protect them when the loss was uncovered. Question: Would I, had I imagined what would happen when the bank losses were uncovered, have done anything different? I thought, and then decided that I would not. The family, Karen and Mark, Arlie and Gary, are strong enough, well educated enough, flexible enough to have choices and freedoms. They are a world away from Mami and Papi. I saw every day how fragile and frightened and vulnerable my sweet souls were, those parents who were more like my children. I was vulnerable as well, vulnerable but not sweet—not sweet at all.

I lie down on top of the place where the gold is buried and wait to be separated by rains and snows and percolated down through the soil to where the treasure is. I know now why I have not been joined by all the hundreds of dead, here, in the Valley. Interest fades. The Bible says that love is stronger than death. So is hate. Hate has kept me here, but I won't burn in my grave, searing the fingers of the people who find this cache. My name won't be anywhere. Theirs will: Ernestine Higgins, Marshall Higgins, all in gold.

MEET THE AUTHOR:
JOANNE GREENBERG

Interviewed by James McManis

James: I suppose we will start with the obvious.

Joanne: Why did I write this book? One of my biggest sources of happiness, of which there are plenty, is gratitude. And I started to think about that. And then I started to think about what gratitude is about, and part of it is about mastery.

Gifts or talents that you use make you grateful. Deep study of anything makes you grateful. And then I thought about the fact that in giving people things, or even saving somebody, gratitude gets very much more difficult. It's harder for the welfare recipient to be grateful when there is no reciprocity. The giver tends to say: "I'm giving you all this stuff, why are you so angry?" So then I thought I'd play it out, so I did.

James: I have heard it said, attributed to Malcolm Gladwell, who claims that you're not an expert or a master until you've clocked 10,000 hours at something. At any task. Do you think that could be said about gratitude? Is it that amount of thinking? Is it a matter of experience?

Joanne: It's more than 10,000 hours. John D. MacDonald says that for writers there's a million words in and a million words out before a writer is ready, but I'm supremely talented so that was 999,950. (Laughs.)

James: I guess in that mindset, is this a story you could have told as well 30 or 40 years ago?

Joanne: Probably not. Few writers back then told the story through dead people.

My niece said, when I gave her my story called *Geography,* a story which I happen to like, she said, "People don't write that way anymore." And they probably don't.

I suppose what we're talking about today is really the change from analog to digital and it's another way of looking at the whole world. I use computers, I hate them and they hate me.

People like to brag to me about, "Well I've got a 90-year-old father and he does the computer every day and he loves the computer." And I say, "Does he spin? Does he weave? Does he can food? Does he make soap and candles and wine? No. I do." It's that world that's incomprehensible to me. I hope I'm not giving this book to the wind because of it.

James: Do you think that something is lost in keeping with gratitude when we interact in the world this way, through technology, rather than with each other? I certainly think that there's a barrier here (pointing to phone), maybe not necessarily viewed as such, that changes things.

Joanne: A sense of community makes a person grateful, also. One is the difference between city and country, or suburb, the people I listen to on TV who are always talking about diversity. We used to be diverse. We used to have rich people and poor people. Right here. Our neighbors. Where our kids grew up, the bank manager was next to a prospector.

You want something incomprehensible to me; it's your music. Bang, scream. Bang, scream. You lose the words. They have to publish the words or you're not going to get the words. I used to be an EMT for rock groups. Out of Folsom Field, which held 80,000 people, and it could be very moving. I watched Heart; and nobody was listening to the music, they were singing. They were all singing. They all knew the words, and 80,000 people were singing, and it blew me away.

James: I like all kinds of music, but there was this album this year, the man's name is Chance the Rapper and he had rap verses, but it was also a very Gospel-heavy album which was interesting.

Joanne: I love that.

James: So I listened to the album and I streamed it online and I said, "I want to buy this. You know, I want to give him my money for this because it was great." And I found out that he doesn't do that, he doesn't make albums. The way I listened to it was the way he gives it to the world. He submits it all online, because for him, it's "how many people can hear this?"

Joanne: I think it's religious. I don't charge for teaching Hebrew.

James: That is interesting, I never thought of it that way.

Joanne: Not that the language is sacred, it's a mitzvah. "Mitzvah" is an interesting Hebrew word. People think it means "good deed," but it doesn't. It means "commandment." We're supposed to do good stuff.

James: So did your faith impact this novel? Was it part of it at all?

Joanne: Well everything, is part of it, but there are no Jews in the book. In this book, this lady, Lily, has no gratitude whatsoever, and when she's dead she's still angry and can't let go. My belief is that there's an afterlife, but it's not what we think it is. And she's not ready for that yet.

James: How long did it take you to write this, or a novel in general?

Joanne: Novels take three years, standard. By the time you get through with all the revising and re-revising, and by the last revision you don't even know what you've written anymore.

James: And do you do one at a time? You have an idea and you just need to get it out?

Joanne: Start to finish. Many people do it differently. I know one writer who writes high points and then fills it in. I don't understand that. Some write the end first. I don't know what the end is!

And, I suppose I'm abstracting my own thoughts. When I see God be surprised at how it all ended up I think, look at Einstein, or look at any of the big thinkers. Dig up Newton, "I had no idea how this was going to end up." Or look at Freud: "I never said that! What the hell is that? Who said that?"

James: Is there anything on the horizon that you are looking at now? Any ideas that you want to tease out or mention?

Joanne: Oh yeah. What I'm working on now, writing, even fiction writing is reactive. Something in the environment needs something I have to say, and I need to learn it. Both elements have to be there.

When I started out in the lit biz, it was an entirely different business. Allow me to present an example to you: Every Christmas, when you had written something, you would get that book leather-bound, gold-embossed. You would get a Christmas card from your publishing company, which was a unique card for the company made by their in-house poet, or Robert Frost, or somebody good, and illustrated by their top illustrator, which was a thing to keep forever.

You got invited to New York. I had a lovely editor, Rob Cowley, who was married to John Cheever's daughter and was the son of Malcolm Cowley. You may not know the name, but he was the greatest in publishing and sponsoring the top writers of the 20th Century. And Rob Cowley and I were walking down the street with another man. And this man said to me, "Did you grow up in a literary family?" And I said, "No I didn't. My father spoke a very lovely Yiddish and he loved jokes and stories and stuff, but actually no, I wouldn't say we were readers."

And then he said to Rob Cowley, "I always wondered what it was like to have in an ordinary day Hemingway, Steinbeck, Dos Pasos, and Gertrude Stein at your table for dinner or for sandwiches, to have all of these exceptional people…"

And Cowley said something like "Yes, if you're interested in watching people slash each other's livers. If you're interested in watching people savage each other. If you're watching displays of stunning egotism and selfishness, yes I guess it was very interesting."

We're not a nice bunch. Why is that? It's a mystery to me. Maybe we have to have a certain amount of selfishness to assume that people will be interested in what we have to say, and a certain amount of egotism to keep going through all the rejections.

James: Maybe in regards to how much it takes out of you…

Because it's exhausting, is it not? Creation is not easy.

Joanne: Well, but look at doing the three to mid-shift in a busy E.R.

We want to be famous, and we're not. I'm very happy. One of my writer friends is my ideal in that. I never heard her say, "How come my book is as good as her book, and she's famous and I'm not?"

I don't say that either, but there was a time maybe 50 years ago when I did. All my writer friend wants to do is write her books, that's all. And they let her do that. They're letting me do that! Most of the writing friends I have are lost in those wishes.

For example, Stephen King was being interviewed once and he said that he had always admired a certain writer, who was his ideal. And he said, "I wrote my first book and I got money. And I found out who his agent was and I called his agent and said 'I would like to entertain him in the city and I would like him to come.' And the agent said, 'He never goes anywhere.'"

Stephen King said, "I wrote more books and then I got enough money to do whatever I wanted, and I called his agent again and I said the day he flies in, his choice of restaurant, whatever. Finest hotel, whatever he would like." And he said "Yes, he would come." Stephen King said the man came in and he was a bigoted, narrow, ugly, wretched back-biting slob, and he said in about 15 minutes he was the sorriest man on Earth who had to spend the rest of this day with this potato.

James: So the longing for fame -- is it affecting the work then? Does it become detrimental to the craft itself?

Joanne: I think so. There's a terrific paradox in this whole thing, and that is that you want to step away so that you can see inward to write. You want to give up your day job and you want to write. But then you're like Antaeus without contact with the world, you're pulled away from your nourishing roots.

At this point in the interview, Joanne's husband calls to her from the kitchen.

Joanne: Well, Albert wants pie.

James: Thank you so much.

James McManis is a freelance writer who specializes in the near-fine dining around the Twin Cities. A former rail jockey and part-time film blogger, he enjoys interviewing juggernauts of American literature. If but a shred of their talent is contagious, he will be able to upgrade to fine dining with his wife around town.

Made in the USA
Middletown, DE
25 November 2017